UNDER THE FLOWERS

BOOK 3 IN THE WINDCATCHER SERIES

Donald Hofstetter

TAZLINA GLACIER
PUBLISHING

First Edition, 2019
ISBN 978-0-9970058-5-1
Tazlina Glacier Publishing
PO Box 717
Glennallen, AK 99588
http://www.tazlinaglacier.com

Cover design by:
Andrei Bat via 99 designs
https://99designs.com/profiles/bandrei

Acknowledgements

Don was very thankful for the friends whose support was invaluable in writing this book, and the whole Windcatcher series. Special thanks to Mary Ann Ward for her editing, Clarence Catledge for sharing his knowledge of guns, Graham Ward for confirming many details, and Teddy Short for always being his biggest supporter.

Don's grandchildren were his greatest joy, and his inspiration for writing. This book is dedicated to every one of them.

"Anyone ever die in here?" Asked Dexter. He was whispering.

No one either knew or was willing to explain anything.

"Where did that come from?" Asked Joseph.

No one answered. Then it came again. Someone was calling for help from somewhere distant-sounding. They were about to make tracks when the floor suddenly vibrated with the impact of something solid. The boom was impossible to miss. The sound combined with the vibration in the floor made everyone jump. Then it happened again — boom, boom, boom! It was under their feet.

"This floor is solid stone," said Dennis in a bit of a panicked voice. "Nothing could live under there."

TABLE OF CONTENTS

CHAPTER 1

THE DAY SETH JACKSON DISAPPEARED

When it's early summer in Idaho, the sagebrush is blooming, aspen trees have new leaves, and cottonwood is ready to go to seed. In the open meadow, the grass is fresh and sage hens are looking for nesting material. Everyone is ready to start another hot Idaho summer. Well, almost everyone.

Seth Jackson was digging a grave. The fella they were planning on putting in that grave wasn't ready for anything in this life. He was wherever old prospectors go when they have worn out their welcome on earth. Only this one was not that old yet, but he was a lot older than he should have been. It's amazing how fast eighty grains of lead ages a man.

Seth got paid five dollars to dig a grave. No one else wanted to. They were all planning to get rich panning gold in the Clearwater River. That's the river the small town of Cougar Rock was built on. If you follow that river you will find the Oxbow River on the other side of town, a few miles upstream. Farther up from there, in the headwaters of the Clearwater, lots of other miners are digging.

Cougar Rock was a small town in a big land. The time was early in the twentieth century and cars are a strange sight, and not always a welcome one yet, but now and then one shows up.

To find this little piece of paradise you would need to head up the Clearwater from Bear Valley. The road narrows and hugs the river for a few miles and gets a little rocky. It wanders through tall pine and fir trees and sees no end to the sweet-smelling sagebrush that grows among the trees, like the buffalo grass and meadow grass that provides pasture for everything that lives there. Fresh clean water flows past deep and clear, and the Chinook salmon are just starting their run. Steelhead won't be far behind.

Indian paintbrush, bluebells and lupine dress the land in wonder and scent. Their new blue heads stand in the knee-high green grass as if they just came from some good hiding place in a child's game of hide and seek.

Farther down the dusty little road, and dead in the middle, there stands a ponderosa that might be more than 500 years old. The road goes up to that tree and then turns a hard right and goes around it. It turns back to the left again on the other side. Nailed to that tree on a tamarack board is a sign that reads. "Welcome to Cougar Rock, population unknown." The tree serves as a sort of gate, with large rock and heavy brush on its left, and the river on the right. The road squeezes by with just enough room for a freight wagon to go past.

In the street the road becomes, a town appears. It

used to be a quiet little town. So quiet that people in the rest of Idaho didn't even know it was there. It was small but growing fast. On the left as you entered, was a saloon, across from that a stable, and then a street that led to the old crossing of the river. Now that gold had been discovered, the main street was becoming a highway for horses.

On that same corner was the blacksmith shop. It was across the main street from the morgue and next to that was a street that looped around the general store. Farther up was a residential street and then a rather rundown hotel and across from it the mill. Other structures and houses were in the process of being built or were in the planning stage.

Freight wagons came and went every few days from the mill to new projects or on down to Bear Valley.

Out in the cemetery, Seth Jackson was busy about his grave project. He was a strong young man who had outgrown his wool pants and every muscle in his lower body was pushing for more room. He had on a brown shirt, and wore a hat that was worn out when he found it. It was blowing across the high desert grass like a tumbleweed in the Idaho wind, a few years before. His curly jet-black hair had long ago sprouted out from under it, and looked a little like a wooly head wrap of some sort.

Seth was what people would call black. The truth was that he was more the color of a mink shawl. His eyes were just a little darker than his skin and were sharp and alert. He was growing fast and already stood just under six feet. He was broad in the shoulders and for fifteen years old he was ahead of his time mentally.

His father was educating him in as much math and English as he knew, but other than that he was not well educated. The other things one might say about Seth were that he was young, strong and hungry. Mostly hungry.

His mother died in a failed attempt to deliver a sibling he never met, and he and his father had been alone ever since.

Other than crop farming, mining was all his father, Dexter Jackson, knew. It scarcely made enough to keep them alive, so any extra money Seth could make was a welcome thing. Today his father was on a river bar about one mile upstream from where the cemetery was. Seth had left him there in the early morning just as the sun was getting ready to make its grand appearance over the mountains to start warming things up.

Seth looked back one last time as the river gained more light. He was rounding a bend in the river with his spud bar and shovel in hand.

There were other men on the same bar, but his father stood out from all the rest and was easy to spot. He was six feet eight and weighed over three hundred pounds. Dexter could use a gun and kept one handy, but up till now, he had gotten by with his fist. He was an easy-going man, but when you're a black man at the turn of the century and you travel alone, you better be good at something, and he was. He looked like he could kick-start a freight train, and he was as quick as a wild pig.

He was working the edge of the bar in his worn-out coveralls and red Johnny top. His hat, which had no definable shape to the brim, was pulled down in the front to block the rising morning sun and his badly worn boots were already wet. Dexter had not touched his face with a razor since the day he was born. He cropped his beard with a sharp knife when it got long enough to get in his way.

That was what Seth remembered and was thinking about when he raised his spud bar for one more almost fruitless stab at the hardpan under his feet. It was a clay-like substance with the constancy of concrete.

He was thinking of what he could buy for an evening meal for him and his father, with the money he would make from his work. Just as he was about to throw the heavy steel tip into the pan, he noticed something in the sky over town, something that caught his attention and caused him to put the bar down for a better look.

A huge cloud of smoke was racing upward down in Cougar Rock. It was rolling the way smoke does when it's being chased by a lot of hot flame in a rather large fire. He watched it a little and thought that he would like to go see what was going on, but he only had a few more inches to go so he decided to stay and finish. No point in making two trips when one would do.

If someone had been watching Seth that day they would have seen a very strange thing indeed. The prairie grass was moving slightly in a southern breeze. The pine trees were starting to sway a little, and a strong young man was digging a hole. His head and the top of his shoulders could be seen sticking out of the ground. There were grave markers, most of wood, that were scattered up the sloping hill behind him. To see it, things appeared as they should. The mound of dirt he had created was on the other side of the hole from town. He watched as the heavy smoke rose higher and faster.

Without taking his eyes off the column of smoke

in the distance, his arms lifted the spud bar. Every muscle in his upper body flexed as he threw the twenty-five-pound shaft of steel as hard as he could into the bottom of the hole. Guiding the bar as it slid through his left hand he let it fly at full speed to a spot in the corner of the hole. The sharp sound it made told him he had hit something even more solid than hardpan. And then, without another sound, Seth disappeared.

The world didn't seem to notice at all. The meadow grass and wildflowers swayed gently in the breeze as if keeping time to some old gospel tune. The pine bows moaned quietly on the hill as little gusts of wind slipped through their needles and a meadowlark sang out from some hiding place in the distance. It was as if Seth had never existed in the first place. He was gone, and nobody knew.

CHAPTER 2

WHERE THERE IS SMOKE THERE IS FIRE

In the town of Cougar Rock, the streets were littered with panicked people. Horse carts ran for the outer edge of town or tried to carry water up from the river. People with buckets of water ran from the millpond across the street from the fire. A workforce was beginning to develop. Without any defined leader, people acted as if they had played this game before. The chaos was already beginning to become organized.

From the roof of a tall building, like the saloon perhaps, the scene might have resembled an anthill that had been kicked open. Half-naked tenants of the hotel were streaming out the open door and into the street.

The West Branch Hotel was on fire. The fire appeared to have started in one of the rooms at the back of the hotel and was already burning hot before it was discovered. Breakfast was not quite over for some people and they were caught totally by surprise.

Pine wood rots very slowly and some trees have been unearthed that had been dead for a very long time. For that reason, and due to its plentiful supply, most structures in town were made of it. One of the biggest problems with pine is that once dried it burns like fuel oil. The entire hotel was made of pine and the back wall was a raging torrent of flame and smoke before the first water hit the hissing boards that added steam to the cloud of smoke billowing into the summer sky.

A newly installed town whistle converted from a steam whistle off a train in Boise, began screaming as soon as word got to the Valley Saw Works across the street. It was fired by steam that was generated by the kiln driers of the mill that were constantly burning, fueled by mill waste from the mill.

Horses, panicked by the sudden sound of the shrill whistle, bolted and tried to run. A wagon with a runaway team crashed down Main Street at break-neck speed. Horses tied to hitching posts either tan-gled in a panicked scramble or pulled free and ran. A miner was thrown off the back of a bucking horse and tumbled into a sliding pile as his horse contin-ued on down the street bucking off everything it had tied to it.

By the time word got out about what caused the whistle, the fire had gotten a good start. Valley Saw Works mill yard across the street had a millpond where water could be obtained. The pond was sup-plied by water from the Clearwater.

Lines of people young and old strung out across the street to the pond, and buckets were handed off back and forth. It was one of those community events that never failed to draw volunteers. In a way, it was a little amazing. People who often didn't even get along stood side by side as if they had been trained to work together. Bucket after bucket crossed the street and in the course of time, the fire began to die down. By mid-afternoon, all that remained were small wisps of smoke. Blackened lumber and ash marked the place where a large part of the rear of the building once stood. Missing boards left holes in the blackened wall that was once the end of the hotel.

Larry Adams stood in the street and stared in disbelief at the smoke smeared windows of what was once his hotel. He had been having a hard time with things all year. The building was old, and what water lines there were had frozen at least once and many leaked even after repair. Renters were often prospectors who only paid if they had the money, and fights that damaged property were common. Now a fire; it was the last straw. The plot the hotel stood on was now worth more than the hotel itself.

Talon stood in the round corral and looked across the river to the house. It was a fine piece of work. He had built the new cabin over the old one. The cave opening had become a black hole to Aggie. She wasn't satisfied until he had replaced the old wood door with a solid iron door that could be locked from the outside.

The new house had a balcony that stretched the full distance of the house and was on the second floor. Aggie liked the view better from there and had the kitchen and living area built up there. The sleeping rooms were on the ground floor. It also had a wrap-around porch that was under the balcony and was about twelve feet wide. It was a new home, only about three years old and made of pine. He noticed it was getting time to oil the siding again. Other than that, it was just what they needed. It was private and tucked away from the rest of the world.

He had also built a new bridge over the Clearwater to land on the other side that he had bought from Ace Valley. He could see the house and front meadow from the barn and working corral on the other side of the river.

Talon was on the other side of the river from home when he noticed the smoke. It rose above the pines and clouded the sky. It was blowing in his direction and at first, he worried that it might be a wildfire. An hour or so had passed before he could smell it.

The smoke wasn't just pine. It had other smells in it that suggested it might be someone's home. Whatever it was, it was a large fire. He had built a rather nice barn and round corral just across the river from the house and from the balcony of the house Aggie and his three-year-old son Reed could see him working most of the time. Today he had been working a young mare of the Nez Perce blood he bought from Tony Blackhawk.

He looked over at the house to see if Aggie had

seen the smoke, but she was busy inside. Reed was watching him from the balcony. Aggie wouldn't be far away because she already knew Reed could, and would, climb the banister rail if he got the chance.

Talon waited in the middle of the round corral to see if she would show up. He faintly heard Reed yell something that included "Mommy" and in an instant, she was on the balcony looking his way. It had become a great way to get her attention if he needed it. He just stood in one spot and watched the house for a minute. The ever watchful eyes of Reed would see him soon enough and call for Mom.

When she was in sight and looking his way he pointed to the smoke in the sky. Aggie watched it rise from the direction of town and then looked back to Talon. From five miles away it was impossible to tell anything about it but it was a worrisome thing, and now alerted to it, they would both watch for advancements. The obvious fear was that it might be a wildfire or become one. Aggie was in a better place to watch from than Talon and would come down and get him if she thought it necessary.

Talon went back to work on the mare and for a while forgot the smoke. He had found a strong market for the Appaloosa horses in Bear Valley and had even sold some in Cougar Rock. Ace Valley had discovered them and liked how they worked. They were smart and strong and could go all day at hard work if he needed them to.

The smoke died down and by late afternoon it was all but gone. Talon knew something had happened and that night decided to ride into town in the morning.

CHAPTER 3

THE VOICE CALLING OUT

FROM THE GRAVE

Talon and Aggie arrived in town the next morning around ten and headed for the general store. Long before they got there they passed the only hotel in town. Black smoke had covered the windows enough that the place looked empty and abandoned.

Most of the building was still intact and standing strong but the fire had damaged it to the point that the rooms were not usable. A few buckets still lay along the edge of the street near the boardwalk out front.

The streets had come to life a couple hours ago and people were inspecting the damage and trying to decide what had happened. Up and down the main street, wagons and saddle horses rattled by. Reed watched the hustle of the everyday lives in the little city from the seat of the wagon while Talon went to see the back of the hotel.

Joseph Long was standing with some other business owners when he got back there. They said "Hi" to Talon and then went on talking. Talon listened to see if he could learn what had happened. No one seemed to know. What they had decided was that it was vandalism.

Larry Adams, owner of the West Branch, was standing with them. He looked flustered and a little defeated. He decided he needed some thinking time. "I'm going down to the saloon," he said. "If anyone needs me, that's where I'll be." He took one more look and started for the saloon.

"Who would do something like this?" asked Talon.

"Who knows," said Joseph, "but it ain't some-thing you would expect to see in Cougar Rock. If this sort of thing is what happens to growing towns, then I think I like the old way better."

The men had moved out to the street and were still talking about the fire when Dexter Jackson rode up. He was easy to spot. Not only was the man as big as a barn, he was the only one who ever rode a Belgian. They were draft horses too wide for most men to sit astride all day. Dexter looked worried. He wasn't a well-known man in town and had only been there a few months. Dexter and his son Seth were for the most part prospectors. They were also the only black people in town and that made them more noticeable.

Dexter rode up to the front of the hotel and dis-mounted like he meant to go inside. He tied the draft horse to the hitching post and looked around. Talon was watching him and he noticed Talon so he walked over.

"Mornin," said Talon.

Dexter looked a little disheveled. That was how he normally looked to Talon. His hat and clothes were still holding mud and sand from his work the day before. He had a wide belt and homespun trousers but his shirt was only a red long john top. He had a heavy beard and Talon noticed for the first time that he had an earring in his left ear. The earring had been bonded while on his ear and could not be removed. It looked like silver. His normally alert, large brown eyes were downcast and his forehead was wrinkled. He had a very worried look about his eyes and face. He took off his hat and held it to his chest as he was walking up. It was a sort of respect thing that Talon never really understood but was afraid to ask.

Dexter was a good bit taller than Talon and he was considerably larger built. Fortunately, he was one of those gentle giants that don't have anything to prove. That was one of the good things about him.

Talon didn't really know him well but he had spoken to Dexter a few times on his way to the headwaters when he started looking for better gravel to work in. He usually stopped by the round corral if he saw Talon working there. He liked to talk horses and seemed to know a good bit about them. He was always jovial around Talon, but in spite of his gentle nature, there seemed to be something under the surface you wouldn't want to press.

Dexter always looked like he had outgrown his clothes. Even his hat seemed a little small.

"Mornin," Dexter said back, "I was just wondering if some of you folk could help me. I lost my boy. He never came in last night. He went to dig a grave for Mr. Johnson but he never came back to camp after that. The grave is there. I saw the dirt when I passed by, but that's all. Seth ain't there. You ain't seen him have you?"

All the men looked at each other. No one said anything for a few seconds. Joseph was the first to speak.

"Well, I guess I ain't seen him since the other day. It was late. He had him a spud bar and shovel

23

he got from somewhere and was headed out towards your claim. But ain't seen him since then."

Dennis Caldwell had been one of the men in the first circle when Talon had showed up. "Ain't this about a mess," he said. "First we got our only hotel in ashes, besides that somebody up and shoots a stranger. Now the fella digging the grave has gone missing. If this keeps up, my stable could be the next thing to go up in smoke. Makes me glad I got insurance. This is getting a lot bigger than our volunteer night watchers. This is looking like we need an actual sheriff. I been saying that all along. Maybe now people will listen. This little town is growing way too fast. We don't even have a jail anymore now that the hotel burned down. Was anybody in there by the way, when it happened?"

No one seemed to know that either. They all just stood looking at each other a little bewildered like.

"Maybe we ought to take a look," said Joseph.

The five men carefully entered the front door of the smoke-stained hotel and walked through the twenty-four-foot wide lobby. At the back of the lobby was a large door, and behind that there was another large room with a back door that exited the building to the alley behind it.

As soon as they entered the first door, light from the missing rear wallboards showed them what they had come to see. On their right as they came in was a steel bar door with a heavy chain and lock to keep it closed. Behind the door was a dead end natural shaft. It was where one of the lava tubes had stopped and left no way out. The walls and part of the floor were flow rock from the Yellowstone volcanic era. High-pressure eruptions that caused the lava tubes under Idaho in the first place had carved the ground under most of the area into caves that had blown through a natural cave system already there, resulting in an anthill effect inside the mountain where Cougar Rock had been built.

The tubes were everywhere. This one had been used for a jail since the town was new. At one point it had been longer and ran along the hillside the hotel was built into. The builders cut it off to make room for the hotel. The short piece left behind had a two-foot thick stone wall built across it to seal it off and a jail-type door three feet wide had been cemented into the wall. From inside the jail, the only thing that could be seen was whatever was in front of the door.

In the heat of summer, it was a good place to be, because the temperature was always cool in the shaft, even when it climbed to over a hundred outside. Now and then night watchers used it to escape the night heat and rest for a little while. Night watchers were so called because they volunteered to try to keep watch over the town at night. When Cougar Rock was small it was a great idea for the town and was cheap. But those days had just ended.

One of the men tried the lock when he got to the door. It was locked.

"Anybody in there?" He called out.

No answer came back.

"Better have a look," said Joseph. "Smoke could

have left someone in bad shape." On the wall not far from the door was the key to the lock. The men entered the natural cell and couldn't see anything. It had no light. Dexter noticed a lamp on the counter on the way in and retrieved it. From his pocket, he produced a stick match. He struck it with the edge of his thumbnail and lit the lantern.

Inside, the cell was empty. Smoke had added to the unsavory sight of the place and added a dusting on the cot mattress with a sooty black stain. The walls were scarred from graffiti and tobacco spit and the cell smelled of old urine. Part of the floor at the closed end was dirt and had been dug into by past prisoners trying to escape. The digging always stopped when they ran into rock.

Aggie had hassled Talon into wearing his best clothes. They were the ones that were made for him a few years ago on his way to his new life and he worried about them as soon as he entered the cell. The stone grey tailored pants and bright red plaid shirt were important to him and he kept inspecting them. He had a new pair of boots as well. He bought those from Joseph Long at the store. They made him look like a regular dandy but they also made him feel rich. Aggie liked how he looked in them and made him wear them any time she could.

The other men were dressed mostly in cotton dungarees. They were Levi Strauss and anyone who could afford them wore them. Talon wished he still had his on.

He was glad Aggie was still outside. This wasn't a place he would have liked her to see, or to smell for that matter. He walked over to the dirt part of the floor and in the dim light of the lantern looked for tracks or maybe a temporary grave someone might have dug to get away from the smoke. The floor had tracks but they appeared to be old. On all the broken rock piled in the end of the shaft and on the walls were the names of dismally bored prisoners. Some were in pencil and hard to read but others were scrawled in the white chalky marks left by the alkali that was scaled onto some of the rocks. The place had a very depressing spirit to it and looked more like Satan's torture chamber than a place to keep people in. It smelled even worse.

"How long has this place been a jail?" Talon asked.

"Long as the town's been here," said Joseph. "It was here before the hotel was built. They tell me the shaft was a good bit longer back then. They cut it off to build the hotel. That's when they put this wall here in. The other one that was at the old entrance was taken down and the rock used for this one. The jail's been here longer than the hotel."

Joseph could see the disgust on Talon's face.

"Now and then," Joseph quickly added, "someone throws a bucket of water on the floor where there's stone and tries to help the smell, but it ain't worth much. We need a new one now."

Talon couldn't have agreed more. They looked a little longer, decided it was empty, and walked out into the back of the hotel again. The floor there was also flow rock. Over the rock had been layered

sawdust that had decomposed into dirt. More sawdust had been added until the floor was about four
inches deep in old dust and chips. It was a large room
of about twenty-four feet square. The walls were
pine that had been cemented down to the stone floor.

The sound of the jail door closing sent a little
chill down Talon's spine as he stood in the dim light
coming in from the fire damaged hole in the rear of
the room. The place would have been a little spooky
to him even without the cell. Dust clung to the walls
and hung like cobwebs from the ceiling joists. In one
corner were some old kegs that looked empty. A little trash had been tossed onto the floor and left lay.
The smell of the cell was still present even six feet
from the door. There were no windows anywhere in
the room and soot from the fire had added a black
film that hung on everything.

He stood for a moment with the other men and
was ready to leave when he saw Dexter by the door.
He had forgotten about Dexter. He had been in the
cell but only in a couple feet and then went out to

wait by the exit door. His eyes were open wide and he was still holding his hat.

Talon wanted to say something but he wasn't sure what it should be. For an instant the room was silent. Someone walked past the hole out in the alley and everyone looked in that direction.

"Well," said Dennis.

"Hush," Talon interrupted.

"Say what?" questioned Dennis.

"Be quiet." Said Talon. He raised his hand to face Dennis.

Dennis looked over at Joseph. He wasn't used to being told what to do, especially being told to shut up. He didn't know if he should be offended or not, but he decided to wait it out and see.

"There it is again," Said Talon. "Did you hear that?"

Everyone stopped to listen. Talon was the only one who seemed to have heard something, and even he wasn't sure what he heard. In a few seconds, it happened again.

A faint voice was in the room with them. That time they all heard it. It was like something far away that somehow knew they were there, an eerie sound but not one that could be mistaken for anything but a human voice. It seemed to come from everywhere and nowhere. Like a voice one could imagine drifting up from a grave.

Dexter backed a little toward the door. He was staring at the old cell door. His eyes were even bigger than normal and he had his hat wadded up where his huge fist had closed tightly around it.

Talon wanted to head for the door at first himself. He also was watching the cell door. The image of his old cabin door breathing on his feet the first time he saw it came to mind. This, however, was not wind. What he heard was a human voice. The first thing in his mind was that the place was haunted. That old cell could easily have caused that, he reasoned. Everyone stood stock still.

"Anyone ever die in here?" Asked Dexter. He was whispering.

No one either knew or was willing to explain anything.

"Where did that come from?" Asked Joseph.

No one answered. Then it came again. Someone was calling for help from somewhere distant-sounding. They were about to make tracks when the floor suddenly vibrated with the impact of something solid. The boom was impossible to miss. The sound combined with the vibration in the floor made everyone jump. Then it happened again — boom, boom, boom! It was under their feet.

"This floor is solid stone," said Dennis in a bit of a panicked voice. "Nothing could live under there."

That was enough for Dexter. He turned and headed for the door at a deliberate pace. Talon grabbed his shirt as he tried to pass. Boom, boom, boom, went the floor again. Talon realized what Dexter could not have known. There had to be a shaft under the floor that was holding someone.

Dexter stopped when Talon took hold of his shirt and was ready to pull his hand free if anything else happened. He was closest to the door, so he waited just a second more. There wasn't much that Dexter feared, but due to his raising, he feared anything that might get your soul from the other side. He was ready to bolt, and so were some of the other people, when they heard the voice again. It was definitely coming from under their feet. Talon went down on his knees and began scooping away the old chips. Under several inches, he came to stone that was flat for the most part and had little flow marks in it that would have made it nearly impossible to keep clean without the sawdust.

"The floor must be thin here," he said, "I need something to pound with."

It took a moment for the others to realize what Talon was thinking. It was the only thing that made any sense. The door between the lounge and the back room had a dead weight made of lead that pulled the door closed after it had been opened. Dexter, somewhat in spite of his better judgment, cut the rope that the weight was hanging on. He handed it to Talon. The weight of it was around ten pounds. It was the perfect thing. Talon raised it up and slammed it onto the floor.

"Easy there," said Joseph. "If it's thin enough we could all wind up in the devil's locker." Talon looked up at him and was about to say something when the floor sounded again. Boom, boom, boom!

"Help," someone called out from under the floor. The voice was faint but it was easier to hear now that the overburden had been removed. The floor couldn't have been more than a few inches thick at most and the sound of the spud bar hitting the floor again sounded like it was being dropped on the floor from inside the room.

"Can you hear me?" The voice called from below.

"We hear you," called Talon. "Who are you?"

"It's Seth Jackson." The voice called back.

Dexter could hardly believe his ears.

"Seth," he called back, "how'd you get under there, son? Are you okay?"

"Say, is that you Papa? I fell through the grave and can't get out."

"Are you okay?" Dexter repeated.

"No," called Seth, "I'm hungry."

Dexter had also gone to his hands and knees and was calling through the spot Talon had cleared on the floor. He smiled a smile big as a baby moon at Talon.

"He's okay," said Dexter. "He was born hungry." "You get yourself back up to the grave Seth. I be on my way."

Dexter rose to his feet as smooth as an athlete. He patted Talon on the shoulder and without another word disappeared out the door. Without the weight, the door stood open and what light the smoke scum let in was a welcome sight to Talon.

CHAPTER 4

BOILING HOT DOWN BELOW

Seth had fallen on the last drop of his spud bar. It landed with the force of a pile driver in a natural crack. The slab of rock he was standing on was in the ceiling of the lava tube where he had been digging. The bar wedged into the crack and pushed the slab over just enough to loosen it from the edge of rock that had held it for past centuries. The slab turned out to be about four feet square and six inches thick, and it fell without warning.

Ten feet later, Seth hit the bottom of the tube. Dust quickly filled the air and other smaller rock dropped out of the ceiling onto his back and legs. Fortunately, there was enough dirt left in the grave to cover some of him and he was only bruised a little on his back.

At first, he was totally at a loss to understand what had happened to him. The dust settled a little, and the light shown through the grave hole. His first reaction was shock. His hat was gone and his hair was full of dirt from the falling rock. He sat up looked around and wiped the dust from his eyes. From sitting on his knees the hole looked even deeper than it was.

Seth gathered his senses for a moment and realized what had happened. He brushed dust and gravel off his pants and then began trying to figure how to get back out of the hole. The ceiling was way too high to reach from the floor and the walls were too wide apart to be of any use. He thought about calling out but was fairly certain no one would hear him. The graveyard was several hundred yards from town.

He looked up one more time at the light above

and figured he was in there for a while. His father would not miss him till evening and no one else would miss him at all. The ice house in Cougar Rock would keep the body cool for a while more, so not even Alvin Johnson would look for him till late in the day.

He dug around in the rock and dirt and found his hat. It looked as good as it ever had. He put it back on and decided to have a look around. Maybe there was another way out. From where he stood the light let him see only a few yards in either direction from the hole. He thought about things for a little while and decided to head in the direction toward town.

The shaft ran in the direction of town for as far as he could see. He thought it fortunate that it didn't run in some other direction. It was a straight shaft for a long way ahead of him.

In the other direction, it appeared to parallel the river for a ways but it looked like it might not go far or maybe it just turned sharp in the direction of the river. It was too dark to tell much and it didn't seem too important at the moment. His first problem was he was trapped. He had heard that these tunnels were underground all over the place, but like everything you hear, he figured it to be a fable some desperate miner dreamed up. Now he knew. He had heard that People got lost easily in the caves and were never found. *Still,* he thought, *if I don't go past anything that might confuse me, I should be okay.*

At first, the travel was easy. The shaft ran straight and there wasn't much rock in the way. Large pieces of rock lay here and there on the floor, but they left pathways between them. Not knowing what to expect, he kept the spud bar with him and continued forward.

The light from the hole was soon useless. He discovered that if he turned around, he could easily see the light from the hole and that let him see the path he had found behind himself. Soon enough that was gone as well, and he was groping in the dark. He worried that wandering in the dark could be his undoing and wished he could see something around him to know where he was in relation to the hole. But all he had were a few stick matches in his pocket.

A little while later, he had already used all of them but six. He knew he would need more to get back out so he tried to save the rest. Now more curious than concerned, he worked a little way on in the dark.

It was cool and damp in the tube. Damp was not the usual way of lava tubes. They were normally dry. After a while, the dark started getting a little spooky and he lit another match. When the match he was using burned out he sat down on one of the large rocks and tried to decide what he should do next. He had already gone farther than he had matches to go back on, but he had not found any-thing that looked like a way out. He was sitting in the dark when he heard the thing that drove him on. Water was dripping in the shaft not far ahead. It was echoing in the silent cave, and that made it hard to peg for distance, but he decided to just keep going until he found it. His water jug was out on the ground beside the grave and he suddenly felt thirsty.

Saving matches was his greatest concern and for that reason, he decided not to use any until he had to. One careful step at a time he moved forward. A good bit later, he began to notice the air seemed harder to breathe. It was a lot wetter and the floor was getting slippery. He hoped he had found what he was looking for and lit one of the matches.

At first, all he could see was steam. He had been traveling in it for some time without realizing it. To escape some of it he knelt down on one knee and looked hard in front of himself. The light from the match bounced off the water about ten yards ahead. Under his feet was a thin layer of the water that was flowing past him and running down what looked like it might have once been a vent of some kind blown out by the same pressure that made the shaft.

He reached down and felt the water. After traveling thirty feet it was still too hot to hold his hand in. The match burned out and he sat down again on another large rock. The rock he was sitting on was wet, and he felt the warm water soak his pants. He leaned back against the wall the rock was up against and took in the moment.

He couldn't see, but he could feel the warm air. He ran his hand over the rock he was sitting on and found that it was covered in some kind of moss-like growth. He listened for anything other than the sound of the dripping water but nothing else found his ears.

For what it was worth he was really quite comfortable. He folded his arms and let his back rest solid against the wall. Realizing he would have to wait till the end of day anyway he decided to wait it out where he was. The warm wet steam was like a hot bath and he thought of using it. His pants were already wet on the seat anyway. He undressed and laid his clothes out on the rock he had been sitting on. The air was warmer than he realized and he was soon dripping with the mineral-rich water. The water had an odd smell that reminded him of sulfur, but it wasn't strong. It was warm and wet and he wanted to get into it. Moving carefully he crept along the floor on his hands and knees. A few minutes later he stopped. The water was getting deeper but it was also getting too hot to touch, much less bathe in. The water dripped off his face as the steam collected on his skin and reached the dew point. It was a nice feeling. He wished it was a little cooler, but he liked it just the same.

He sat down on the slick wet floor and relaxed. He tried to sit down where he was, but the floor was too hot so he returned to the rock his clothes were on and he leaned his back against it. The slowly cooling water flowed against and under his naked legs. He couldn't see but he decided that other than that this was a great place. The water was far too hot to drink but he didn't feel that thirsty anymore anyway. He was having a nice steam bath and that was enough.

Something woke him a few hours later. It took him a moment to realize where he was and a few more to remember that something had caused him to wake up. What woke him became a lot more clear a few seconds later. He could hear faint voices above him. Someone was outside the shaft over his head. After he realized he had a way out he started rounding up his stuff.

CHAPTER 5

THE TIMES THEY ARE A CHANGIN

Seth realized he was still naked and started trying to sort out his clothes to put them back on. It was then that he realized his mistake. His clothes were soaked by the wet steam. In spite of the warmth of the steam, they felt cold. He knew he had no choice, and began getting dressed anyway. In the dark, it was a bit of a challenge to find his boots. He couldn't remember where he left them. They were not as wet. They had been left on the floor. Next time, Seth told himself, he would leave his clothes farther away from the water.

Soaking wet and a little miserable, he fumbled around in his pocket for a match. Then it dawned on him they were also soaking wet. It took him a lot longer to get to where he could see the light of the hole than he would have used with a light, but enough walking into floor rock got him to where he was able to see it. It was a lot farther away than he expected. His father was already at the grave a few minutes before he got there. He was shivering when he got to the gravesite, and all he wanted to do was find some of that good old Idaho summer sun.

Dexter was shocked at what he saw when he dragged Seth out of the hole with a rope. He was wet and now he was muddy as well but he was happy.

"Bring any food?" He wanted to know.

The town council gathered at the little courthouse for an emergency meeting. The meeting was underway when Dan Lampwick heard of it. He decided to show up to see what was being done about the hotel and the dead man. He had been down to Bear Valley with a load of lumber and brought back supplies for Joseph Long.

Dan was the man who owned the freight wagons that kept Cougar Rock alive, not to mention a lot of other people in business. He was a dark-complected somewhat short man who didn't weigh more than one hundred and sixty pounds and only stood around five feet five. The gun he kept on his hip made him a lot bigger. He was normally a quiet man and set about his life without much notice, but he was a big part of Cougar Rock.

When he got to the courthouse he went in. There were a lot of empty seats and he chose one near the door.

Dennis Caldwell had the floor and was repeating the same line he had been saying for a couple months. Cougar Rock needed a Sheriff. Now he reminded them they also needed a new jail. Ace Valley owned the sawmill and offered the lumber at cost. He even offered to hire town folk to cut and mill the wood and deduct that from the cost. Several people volunteered to help.

As for a sheriff, they were a little lost. If the night watchers were not enough as things were, then they were not enough at all. But how do you find a sheriff?

Dan offered to have a banner put on his freight wagons, but they only went to Bear Valley, or on occasion Boise.

Joseph had a better idea. He asked if the stage line could put one on the stage headed out of state, and he also offered to telegraph the newspapers in some of the larger cities to advertise the need. It was decided what they could pay and the quest was set into motion.

The last item on the new business was the dead man. "We still need a grave," said Alvin Johnson." He won't last much longer even in the ice house. And if anyone knows, it would be considerate of us to have a name for the grave."

Nobody at the meeting knew anything about the dead man. In fact, no one there had even looked to see if they remembered seeing him around town.

"Someone knows," said Talon. "Was he a miner? One of them might know. I'll ask around and see if I can find anyone. But it might be good if folks get a look at him before you put him in the ground even if we don't have a name." The board agreed to look at the corpse and Talon left to do a little snooping.

Aggie wasn't at the meeting. She had gone shopping with Reed. Talon caught up with her at the store. On the way home, Talon told Aggie of the meeting and that he was going to ask around. She asked to go along and Talon drove the wagon upriver into the headwater country.

The day was warm and Seth had dried out. He was still telling his father how nice the hot spring was when Talon and Aggie got to the gravel bar they were working.

Dexter knew who the dead man was by sight but had never talked to him. "I saw that man the morning he was found," Dexter said. "He was face down on the little bar just downstream of town. He had a pan and a pick beside him. I figured him a miner. Never did hear no shootin though. I was fixin to dig a little there, but when I seen him I just left. I was goin to tell someone but another miner there said he would. I moved up here. Don't want no trouble."

That wasn't much to go on, but Dexter looked like he was done talking. It didn't seem he had much more to tell anyway. Talon felt lucky he got that much.

Talon and Aggie worked all the way up into high country that day and nobody else had anything to add to what he heard from Dexter. The dead man seemed to have been around for a couple weeks before he showed up face down on the gravel bar, and that was all anyone on the river knew.

The next day Talon rode into Cougar Rock to report his findings to Alvin. He was the owner of the morgue and was the one who wanted a name. Alvin heard him enter the shop and came out to meet him.

"Talon," he said, "good to see you. Any word on the guy on ice?"

"Not much," said Talon, "I couldn't find a name. The only thing I figured out was that he was doing a little mining just out of town."

"That's too bad," said Alvin. "The boys from the town meeting came by and had a look at him. More than one of them said once they saw him, that he had talked to them about selling them insurance on their businesses. Strange thing is nobody could remember his name. Almost like he avoided saying it, maybe. Why would a miner be trying to sell insurance in the first place? Anyway, don't matter much now don't suppose. Him being dead and all."

"What does matter," said Talon, "is somebody in town shot him. I'll be glad when we can find a sheriff. We need someone who has more experience with these things. The dead guy makes it easy to forget, but the hotel was set on fire by someone who meant to burn it down."

"Well if any of that is connected," said Alvin, "we won't know what, till we have more information."

"True enough," said Talon. "Maybe the signs on Dan's wagons will find someone in the valley who knows a sheriff. Even if he don't it was nice of him to offer to use his wagons that way."

"He's an interesting man," said Alvin. "Don't talk much. Hard to peg a man like that. Stands to reason though. That seems to be one of the traits of your people. Don't mince words much, says what he means, means what he says."

"My people?" said Talon.

"Ya you know, Indian."

"I never realized he was Indian," said Talon. "What nation, do you know?"

"Well according to Louis over at the Anvil, he's Apache. Seems to like Louis. Talks to him when he's working on the wagons. Louis says he's educated. That explains his manner of speech but not much else.

"Louis tells me that Dan's not his real name either. He changed it. Used to have his father's name. The Apache called him Dances Like Fire. Strange name I thought. But you know Indians an all.

"Said a doctor found him when he was a boy. Bout sixteen or so. It was just after the last of the Indian wars. He was beat up bad. They weren't sure they could keep him alive but they did. They were moving up from Utah. Found him lying near the road just this side of the Three Island Crossing at Glenn's Ferry.

"Most folks might have shot him in those days, but you know how doctors are. Took him home, fixed him up, and then sent him to school. I guess he never said how he came into his business. Might a been the same doc. Anyways, thought all that interesting. Guess you just never can tell."

"Guess not," said Talon.

Talon said goodbye and left the morgue. He stood on the boardwalk in front of the morgue trying to figure things out. It seemed like a lot of loose ends to him. Something was missing but he couldn't tell what.

The information he now had about Dan changed how he thought about him. He liked Dan as much as anyone but knowing he was educated made him see him in a different light. He had never met an educated Indian before. It made him wonder if there was anything else about Dan he would find interesting if he knew. One thing he believed about the Apache was that they were not a people who took to being stepped on much. It made him wonder if someone might have stepped on Dan's toes any time recent.

The thought made him feel a little guilty. He was thinking things that may not be true. But he stopped short of accusing him of anything. *Still,* Talon thought, *he's not much afraid and he does carry a gun.* He made a mental note to try to find out what caliber weapon Dan carried. No one had any idea of what caliber killed the insurance man but there might be a chance of finding a brass cartridge near the kill site. There wasn't much hope in that when he thought about it. There was always someone shooting guns off these days. Might be why nobody thought anything about the shot that did the work.

He stepped back into his saddle. For the moment, there was a lot of work at home and he needed to get to it. As he rode out of town he thought on the things he knew. Somebody shot a man and they must have had a reason. If it was a claim jump or a fight someone should have known something. Maybe someone did, thought Talon. Could be, he just hadn't found the right someone.

He decided he would keep one ear to the ground, just in case. He also decided to keep a closer account of the miners that passed his place during the day. They had become like the geese that fly by. He barely knew they were there. It worried him a little that someone was around who had the right stuff to kill a man. He thought of Aggie and Reed. Their safety and happiness was his life and breath. Not to mention his horses. A man like that could steal as well and might even try to kill a man for the right horse. His broodstock was second to none.

Chapter 6

Domingo Wells

Domingo Wells stepped up onto the boardwalk in front of the drugstore in Bozeman Montana. The job he held there was what amounted to a security guard. He didn't like it. He had once been the sheriff of a small town in South Dakota called Wolf Creek. That job ended when he spent about three weeks chasing a man he believed had evidence in a vigilante hanging.

It was a long chase and to cover his position in town he sent a trail hand from the posse back to fill in for him. The trail hand's name was Sam Edgewood.

Some of the evidence the sheriff needed was in the form of the 30-30 the victim of the hanging had used in the shooting that got him hanged. He sent that back with Edgewood for safe keeping.

Sam had never been anything but a trail hand and had Sheriff Wells not been under the gun he would have had a better idea. As it turned out Sam liked being the sheriff. He strutted up and down the main street wearing a badge he found in the top drawer of the sheriff's desk and showing off the 30-30 he had been given charge of.

Wolf Creek was a small town. But the area was rather large and being sheriff is not something he figured he would ever get to do again. It was not a position he took lightly. He had never felt so respected and powerful. In fact, he liked being sheriff so well that he decided he should do something to ensure his short stint as sheriff would be remembered. So he robbed the bank. He even used the 30-30 to do it with and took the money and the rifle and hit the trail.

A few days later Sheriff Wells sent back the man

he should have sent in the first place. Axle Ford arrived back in town and decided to stay in spite of the escaping robber. He figured the sheriff would have to deal with it when he got back. Leaving the town again was not his opinion of a good idea.

The sheriff returned a week or so later and had the evidence from the hanging but needed the rifle that Sam Edgewood had to go with it. He also needed the bank's money back. He managed to get both and the whole mess was cleaned up. In the interim, however, the city fired him and Ford both for leaving the town unprotected.

Sheriff Wells turned in his badge and rode out with Axle Ford to the big state of Montana. He could have gone to pushing cows, but the money for that paid about as well as did the job he took in Bozeman. Both he and Axle Ford had landed in Bozeman, but Axle couldn't find work in the law field and took a job working for the livery.

Every day around the same time, the two men met at the drugstore for lunch and to look for better work. Today was their lucky day. Domingo opened the paper, looked at the want ads and handed the paper to Axle. He was smiling wide and soon enough both men were on their way to Cougar Rock.

The sun was bright, and the air was pushed by a gentle breeze the day Domingo and Axle started the final climb up the road from Bear Valley. Grass hadn't started to dry on the hills yet and sagebrush was just starting to bloom. The dark green bows of the scattered pine trees moved slowly in the quiet breeze and juniper stood out from large chunks of granite where sagebrush and wild rose grew.

A red tail hawk drifted by overhead and small birds scattered in search of a safer place in deeper brush.

The air was rich with the smell of meadow grass and wild skunk cabbage that found its home in small springs that fed the Clearwater River. The hills for as far as could be seen were high and mostly green with grass and scattered quaking aspens and evergreens.

A small patch of aspen rattled in the breeze and caused Domingo to look over at them. There were sage hens on the ground, so well camouflaged that he almost missed them. He noticed a fox not far off watching them as well. Domingo was already falling in love with the land, long before he looked down into the clean cold water of the river. After seeing that, he decided he would have taken the job at half the pay if he had known what a fine place it was to be.

He had heard of the salmon that spawned in the river, and that was more exciting to him than the promise of gold it was said to have. He had become an accomplished fly fisherman over the years, and the thought of hooking into a Chinook salmon had him all but giddy. He could hardly wait to break out his rod and let the games begin.

When the two men entered town you could have picked them out of a crowd without looking twice. They were both dressed in long black oilskin trench coats and black hats. Both were wearing side irons as well. All that was lacking was the badge. A large brown dog trotted out to meet them but offered up no complaint as they started down Main Street.

Crows watched from the tops of buildings and people wandered the streets in every kind of clothes style you could think of. Miners carried supplies on pack horses and rode by without a word.

Overall, it looked like any other small town you could visit. There were no cars or motor vehicles of any kind but wagons and buggies were everywhere. They passed the saloon where another dog lay. It looked older than the first and didn't seem to notice them at all.

Someone sitting in a straight leg chair leaning back against the wall was drinking a beer in the shade of the awning. He nodded when he saw the sheriff. Domingo nodded back.

A woman in a nice green dress walked across the street in front of them and blushed a little when she looked up. She looked like she had been caught at something. She suddenly looked down at the street, raised her dress a little and hurried to the other side. A load of fresh lumber on its way out of town passed by and the driver nodded as well. Dust drifted up behind the wagon and clung to their boots as they passed. Hot sun had turned the street into a dusty path that donated powder for every business or person in town. The breeze sent it up onto the boardwalk and the corners of the windows collected it like dry gray snow.

Domingo and Axle were not the only thing that could not escape notice. The horse Domingo rode was also unique; it was an Overo Paint. Most of its head was white. Except for a small white patch just behind his right front leg, the rest of the horse was the color of a dark bay. It had one glass eye and a well-formed head and ears. It was a horse with unusual conformation and held a good gait. Anyone would have been proud to own him.

Axle's horse was a little heavier built and may have been a Morgan cross. It had a blaze on its forehead and black hooves. It was a solid-looking horse like the kind a farmer could have made use of. Not fast, but strong and well made.

The two men stood out enough that when Joseph Long saw them he knew who they were. He walked down the street to meet them when they pulled up in front of the courthouse.

The jail was well underway when they arrived. It had been custom built by Louis Willis. He was the town blacksmith and he took pride in his work. So much so, that the chances of anyone ever breaking out of his jail were next to none.

The new jail had features the old one lacked. For one thing, it had a latrine. No more marching prisoners out to the outhouse every time they got bored. It also had a light he recessed into the ceiling behind a locked steel grid. The switch was in the cell but had an override switch outside the cell. It had four bunks that folded up against the wall and were built of solid iron that was embedded into the wall to keep them in place. The walls were two feet of solid stone eight feet high, and even the ceiling was laced with iron bars.

The rest of the sheriff's office was still under construction, but the jail was finished. The few town drunks that lived in Cougar Rock were pleased indeed.

Sheriff Domingo Wells and his deputy Axle Ford were sworn in on the same hour they arrived and given badges Joseph had mailed in from Boise. It was a warm clear day at the new county seat in the courthouse, and everyone who knew they were in town was excited to have them.

From there they walked across the street to the new sheriff's office. Once they were settled in they went to the hotel to see the damage. When they came around the corner of the hotel a tall man was flipping over a board, looking for anything that might be a clue to the fire. He had his back turned to them. They stopped ten feet away to watch. When they did, Talon Windcatcher stood up and turned in their direction. Domingo took a step back in surprise. So did Talon. Domingo smiled.

"Didn't mean to disturb your camp," Domingo

said, "not this time anyway."

Talon tipped his hat back and grinned back at him. Axle was standing beside Domingo.

"Oh well," said Talon, "it wasn't a great place to camp anyway." He thought it better not to remind them of what he did to theirs.

It was a sort of reunion. The three men had met before. Talon was the man Domingo chased down for the evidence in the vigilante hanging that ended his job.

"I take it that you live here abouts these days. Should of realized I might run into you. You were headed this direction the last time we saw you. I see you got yourself a new pair of boots."

Talon laughed. "Had to," said Talon, "somebody took the others and rode away."

The three men laughed again.

Talon was not sure what to think. He had not been told that the city had hired a sheriff, much less Domingo Wells, but he put it together as soon as he saw Domingo and Axle in front of him.

He gathered his composure and waited to see what Domingo would do next. He was hoping they didn't think he had anything to do with the fire. He could see Domingo studying his eyes and returned the momentary gaze.

"You don't work for Wolf Creek no more?" asked Talon.

"Long story," said Domingo. "I'll tell you about it some time."

Talon had a hunch that he might not want to know why Domingo and Axle were available for hire. He was just glad they were. He decided to change the subject. "I live up river a little way," said Talon, "I have a family now, and we built our cabin on my land up on the Oxbow."

He gestured with his hand at the hotel. He wanted to explain why he was at the scene. "I was working outside the other day when I saw the smoke. It's about five miles from here. I been working with the city since then to try to find out anything I can about a dead miner they found down on the river. I keep thinking this might be connected."

"Heard about that fella," Domingo said. "But I don't have enough information to make any call yet myself. What makes you think it could be related?"

"Pretty close together," said Talon. "Nothing outside the everyday stuff before and then all at once someone is dead and the hotel goes up the smoke hole."

"Well, me being new to the whole thing leaves me at your mercy, so to speak," Domingo said. "Could be you got something there. Find anything yet?"

"Well, not much," said Talon, "but I can tell you that I am a lot happier to see you now than I was the last time." All three men chuckled a little about that.

"We decided we needed a lot of help around here. I'm glad it was you they hired. You have a way of not giving up easy." The three men laughed again. It was a bit of an inside joke.

"I don't know much about the fire," said Talon," but the shooting was no accident." Talon continued telling Domingo what he had found out about the dead man, and where he had found it. He also told him where he should be able to find Dexter and Seth. He didn't mention anything about Dan Lampwick.

"You see anything here that looks suspicious?" Domingo asked Talon.

Talon looked down at the pile of ashes on the ground at his feet. He was about to say something when a small bright piece of wood caught his eye just outside the edge of the fire. "Not till now," he said.

He had been standing on the good end of a burnt stick match. When he moved his foot he saw it. He bent down and picked it up. After he inspected it for a second he handed it to Domingo. "It ain't much to go on," he said, "since anyone could have dropped it after the fire but it might be something to know about."

"Interesting," said Domingo. He inspected the match and handed it to Axle.

"Axle," said Domingo, "this is Talon. He's the one we dubbed Three Feathers in the hanging case. You never met him."

Axle put out his hand and shook hands with Talon. "Good to meet you," Axle said.

"Same to you," said Talon.

The three men talked a little while longer about the dead man and then went their way. Talon headed for home. Axle wanted to visit the river bar where the body had been recovered. Domingo went back to the office to help finish with the construction.

CHAPTER 7

LOOKING FOR THE LIGHT

AT THE END OF THE TUNNEL

Days are normally slow in places like Cougar Rock. The miners get started around daybreak and the rest of the town starts up not long after.

Domingo waited for the light and set out to have a look at the town and the river. He liked what he had seen so far, but something in him made him feel uneasy anytime he was in a strange place. He would not be satisfied until he had gotten a look at every cubbyhole and potential hiding place in the valley.

He rode down to the crossing and over to the other side of the Clearwater. From there he worked his way up the old trail all the way to the cabin where Aggie's parents lived. He didn't know who they were when he saw the cabin but he didn't care, he was just looking.

He rode all the way up to Talon's cabin and crossed the bridge to head back to town. There was someone working a good-looking horse in the round pen on the other side of the river. He recognized who it was and waited for him to realize he was there. It was Talon Windcatcher. He stopped to say Hi.

"So this is the place you landed," said Domingo, "I wondered about that a few times. I never saw Tony after those days either. He lives around here too, does he?"

"Not far," said Talon, "over on the reservation. I see him all the time. I'll tell him to stop by and see you the next time he is in town."

"I'd like that," said Domingo. "What brought you here? You hear about gold?"

"The cabin," said Talon. "I got it from my people. They thought it had spirits so nobody wanted it. People kept disappearing there. I figured it out the day I found the cave. They were getting lost."

"Lost," said Domingo, "in a cave?"

"Ya, the whole mountain is a cave. A lot of the country around here is tunnels and springs. My cabin was built right over the one I been workin in. I got lost in there myself one time."

Domingo found the idea of a cave interesting. He had already heard about the shaft Seth had found, and now he was learning about another one. It sounded like something he might want to explore.

"Find anything while you were in there?" He wanted to know.

"Gold, and my wife," said Talon. He smiled when he said it.

"A wife, now that's got to be one for the books. The gold I could see, but a wife, now that's different."

Talon explained the cave and how Aggie wound up in it. He also told Domingo about the gold and why he never intended to go back to look for more. It sometimes made him wonder about the gold, but the experience the last time taught him well. He decided once was enough. He had all he needed anyway.

"You wouldn't mind showing me that cave some time would you?" Domingo asked.

"Wouldn't mind at all," said Talon. "If you're up to it, we can have a look right now. You rode all the way out here, might just as well make it worth your ride."

Domingo didn't want to put Talon out, but he was right about the ride. Besides that, the cave was too interesting to turn him down. Talon explained where Aggie's parents lived and how they came out of the cave in his father-in-law's backyard. He also explained why his new cabin was built over the other one and the heavy steel door. As they approached the house, Reed announced their coming and Aggie came out onto the balcony. The first thing Domingo noticed was that she was beautiful. She was wearing a working dress made from light blue cotton. Her long auburn hair fell over her shoulders and lay in loose curls over her breasts. Her eyes were dark and there was something mysterious, even a little wild looking about her. She was with her sister May, who visited a lot and helped out with Reed.

"Will I be setting another plate for lunch?" She wanted to know.

Talon looked over at Domingo.

"Thank you, ma'am, but I was just passin through," Domingo said.

The women just smiled and waved as they went back into the house.

"Really wouldn't mind," said Talon.

"I really need to get back. Lost a job once leaving a town too long."

Talon wondered about that, but he decided to let it lay. They entered the ground floor of the cabin and turned toward the wall of the mountain. Inside another door, they entered the original cabin and Talon unlocked the iron door and lifted it out of the way. He had a lantern hanging on a peg just under the floor and he lit it to light the shaft. The familiar grayish brown stone walls lit up showing the cot he used to sleep on and the gravely floor.

The instant the lamp lit the floor Talon stopped. Domingo had been looking at the natural rock walls and floor and was interested in the fact that the walls were granite. The stone was flecked with quartz and something very small that looked like it might be garnet crystals. When Talon stopped Domingo almost bumped into him.

Talon held the lamp higher and inspected the floor better. There were man tracks in the loose gravel. Without saying anything he moved forward to the stream that he still worked now and then and jumped across it to the other side. Domingo followed. On the other side, Talon walked up the stream to a place where the gravel was mostly sand and there he stopped again. He was inspecting the floor with a careful eye and Domingo noticed.

"Something wrong?" Domingo asked.

He had been looking at the cave and was enjoying the wonder of it. The air was moving and blowing down the small holes the stream moved through. Not far ahead he could see the little bench that Talon had used that had led to the rest of the cave. Talon had stopped again and had said nothing the whole time they were in the cave.

"Ya, I think so," said Talon. "These are not my tracks."

"Do tell," said Domingo. Domingo took that to mean that no one else should be in this part of the cave. Is there another way in that you know of?"

"No way a normal human would be able to use," said Talon.

The cave was silent except for the sound of the little stream and the wind. Talon stood still for a while to listen and then moved on up the shaft. He had followed the stream before and knew that it entered the cave from the floor. It bubbled up from under a solid granite wall of rip-rap that created a dead end in the end of the shaft.

He also knew that there was another small three-foot hole in the side of the shaft that happened to be straight across the shaft from another one just like it on the other side. He remembered that the little bench he once hid on had a shaft that had stalactites that hung down like teeth. It was on the other side of the tunnel he had blocked years ago.

He walked slowly up the little stream holding the lamp in front of him and watching the tracks. The floor became more solid as he went and in a short time, he was standing on solid stone where the tracks disappeared. The stone floor was smooth granite and had little lumps in it. The tiny red stones in the granite glittered in the lamplight as they passed onto the solid floor.

In front of him, the shaft had a low ceiling in one spot that was about eight feet wide which forced him to bend slightly over to pass under it. He had done that before but only with a homemade torch.

With the lantern, the scene was considerably different. The floor was a clean piece of stone with a somewhat wide but shallow stream flowing over it. He noticed that under the low bridge there was a place where sand and pebbles had been deposited, but only in one spot about three feet wide. He stopped there to have a look.

The wind was creating a bit of a moan until he got to the spot. When it suddenly stopped he knew he had found another way in. He was standing in the way of the wind. He looked again at the wall but found nothing. Then he remembered the sand on the floor and went down on one knee so he could get a better look at the ceiling. It wasn't there.

A three-foot natural hole opened above him. He stood up and found that another shaft, a lot like the one he was in, crossed his. It had a sandy floor and he was head and shoulders into it when he stood up. He held the lantern in the new shaft and found that the tracks came down that shaft to the hole. They also crossed the hole and disappeared beyond the reach of his lamp beyond where he was standing.

He could see where someone had jumped over the hole and gone on and then returned to the hole. They also went beyond where he could see in the direction they came from as the person left. Domingo had been silent and just followed Talon until then. He stood in the dark while Talon searched out the hole.

"What's up there?" he wanted to know. Can you see anything?"

"Sand," said Talon. "I see a lot of sand in another shaft. Whoever came here, came this way."

"Think we should follow it?" Domingo asked.

"I've had really bad luck with that," said Talon. "We might be able to track him back, if he don't cross water or walk over a long stretch of stone in an area where other shafts branch off. If he does, or we find that we walked past shafts that joined at a steep angle we failed to see going in, we might be ok. To my thinking, it's way too dangerous to try. Whoever he was might have a safe way in or might not ever find his way out of the cave at all.

"I wonder if he tried the iron door and gave up. He may have been already lost and decided to keep trying after he couldn't get out at our place. Too many people now, someone was bound to get lost in these caves. I hope he gets out."

"I don't think I would worry too much about that," said Domingo. "If he was needing to get out he would have been beating on that door with your pick or a rock until he dropped over. My guess is he thought he knew where he was and didn't want you to know he was here. Was he working your claim do you think?"

"Didn't notice," said Talon, "should check when we get back."

The two men returned to the shaft under the cabin and Talon decided that if the intruder had been jumping his claim he used his own pan and tools. Talon's were where he left them. The stream looked the same also. There was, however, handfuls of sand that had been thrown against the wall wet. They looked like someone had scooped them out of the stream and threw them against the wall without thinking. Like they were looking for something in the stream they never found.

Talon relocked the iron door and the two men went out to the meadow he had for a front yard. The sun felt good and they were glad to be out in the light again. One of the horses wandered over to say Hi. Talon petted her neck and thought about what he had learned in the shaft. Someone knew where his claim was and they were under his house without his knowing.

"I would never have dreamed a place like this could happen anywhere in the world," said Domingo, "How many of these underground tunnels do you think might be here?"

"A lot of them I think," said Talon. "I spent a few days lost in some of them. You can hear wind in shafts so close to the one you are in that if you listen you can hear the sand shifting in the wind against the wall on the other side.

"Sometimes you can be in a cool shaft that has

one wall warmer than the other or you can hear something moving overhead like a stream or small rocks falling in the distance. One place we were in a shaft had walls that felt like glass. Way under it was water falling down some rapids. Sounded like it was a hundred feet below us. We were blessed to get out alive."

"I see why you don't want to go back into it," said Domingo, "I wouldn't want to either, but someone did and we should try to find out who. If they're not still in there they will be back. Assuming they survived, that is."

Talon watched Domingo leave and made sure none of his horses tried to follow him. He worried about the intruder. It was unnerving to him that someone had invaded their privacy, and stood under the house without them knowing. He thought of Aggie and Reed and was glad the iron door was locked from the outside.

Before he returned to the round pen he went upstairs to warn Aggie and to tell her what they saw and of where the intruder entered. Her response was short and wise.

"We need a dog, Talon. You need to find us a dog."

Talon wondered over the tracks the rest of the day. By mid-afternoon, he decided to have a look around. The question kept coming to him of why they were there. Was someone snooping around, or were they just lost in the cave and looking for a way out. He rode the old trail, and on the way back decided to look for any questionable sign of people on the hill overlooking the house. What he found was as concerning as the tracks in the shaft.

Someone had been up on the hill long enough to have left a sort of nest where they sat in the loose earth watching. From where they had been, he could see the house and the round pen. It was a good place to watch from if you wanted to stay hidden. The trail they used worked through willow and underbrush at the bottom, and heavy sage and pine farther up. They had crawled up under a large blue spruce and used the low hanging limbs for a curtain to blind anyone from seeing them from below.

As long as they arrived early and stayed till late there would be very little chance of anyone seeing them. He found where they rode a horse off the trail at a place where there was a little finger of steep land that leveled off a hundred feet or so up from the trail. That spot was a hundred yards or so from the spruce. They had tied the horse there and walked up to the overlook.

Talon checked the tracks the horse left and found some useful information. The horse had one pigeon-toed hoof on the right front. That meant it would throw that hoof out as it walked or ran. "A wing-footed horse," he said out loud.

He also noticed that the man tracks were very similar to the ones in the shaft. The horse had rather large feet but didn't cut an abnormally deep track like a heavy horse might, and it needed its feet trimmed. From the tracks and the abuse the tree took where it had been tied, it looked like the horse had the habit of pulling back on the lead rope to try to break free.

Talon felt he now knew what he might be looking for. In his mind, it would be like an American Horse with one wing foot, and someone about his size, possibly wearing spurs to keep a ruddy animal in tow. If the rider was as dumb as the horse appeared to be, he might also be using a curved bit or worse, even a rolling spoon bit. He hated those bits and had seen them damage a horse's mouth so that you could not get them to take a bit at all anymore. A man wanting fast results could even scoop out part of the roof of a horse's mouth with one of them. Still, if a horse was knot-headed enough, even an experienced rider might be tempted to use one. He would be watching for a horse wearing one. Most horsemen rarely used them. He had seen a lot of horses that pulled back and danced around when they were tied. That in itself might not mean anything, but this horse kept pulling and fighting the lead rope for a long time. The bark was gone where the rope wrapped around the tree, and the ground was chewed up like it had been plowed.

When he had finished reading the news on the ground, he went to the house and retrieved the ax. By the end of the day, that spruce tree was limbed eight feet up the trunk.

Domingo rode back into town with a lot of information he had little idea what to do with. What he did know was that something was going on in the little town of Cougar Rock. Whatever it was wasn't something to be taken lightly. One man was already dead, and he also believed that the hotel fire was arson.

With the whole mountain laced with underground tunnels, a man who wanted to could hide right under someone's feet. Literally under someone's feet. The Clearwater River was braided for a good way, where it passed town and that could also make for hiding places. Little islands had miners camped on most of them, and any one of the camps could be empty and not be recognized as an abandoned camp. He made a mental note to put Axle to work on the dead man. He would keep to town and work on the hotel.

CHAPTER 8
WAS IT A PROMISE OR A THREAT?

Ed Clanton had been trying to sell his ranch for longer than he expected, but the wait enlarged the herd and allowed for a better price. He had promised his soon-to-be ex-wife and his daughter that when he sold he would split the money evenly between the three of them and they could all go their separate ways.

His daughter's name was Lacey and she was his only child.

So, when he did sell, he gave the buyer a little break in trade for giving him twenty percent of the price in cash. That kept Janice from complaining when he gave Lacey a good bit more than he kept or gave to Janice.

Lacey rode into town with her parents with a somewhat smaller saddle horse in tow. She bought herself a brand new buggy. She had it sent in from the big city of Bozeman Montana before the ranch ever sold.

Lacey made a promise the day Talon left her father's ranch, where he worked for a while. Or maybe it was more like a threat. In any case, when he told her she couldn't go with him, she said that if he didn't take her she would just follow him wherever he went. She tried to do that very thing the day after he left, but things were not in her favor. She did swing a pretty good deal in the process.

That was five years ago. Now she was making good on her promise. Lacey knew where she wanted to go, and she thought she knew how to get there. What she didn't know was where "there" was. That was information she planned to get from Sheriff

Wells. He was the last one to see Talon, and he knew the direction to go to find him.

Her first stop was Wolf Creek. Domingo was gone, but the county seat knew where his last letter of reference went, so it was off to Bozeman.

She had the foresight to get her mother to build her clothes for the trip. Her mother was a seamstress, and a good one. Lacey asked for a pair of culottes made from black cotton denim. She wanted them to go all the way down to the tops of her boots and she wanted a green plaid shirt to wear with it. She braided her hair in two long braids and wrapped them around the top of her head. Over that, she pushed on a man's western style hat. She wanted the hat to look used so she found a trail hand with a nice used-looking hat she wanted and traded him out of it with a new one. The idea was to look like a man at any distance and that's how she looked.

She set out from Wolf Creek on a wet day. The sky was dark and cold. There was a little sleet in the rain. She pulled her coat up tight and flipped up the collar. The wind was blowing for the most part from the back of the buggy for most of the day. Gusts of ice-laden wind slammed into the back of the buggy with enough force to make it felt throughout. Wet snow clung to the brush and laid the sprouting green grass over flat enough to sit on it, and sit on it is what it did. By ten in the morning, the world was as white as a winter day. Melting snow and ice clung to the rump of the pull mare and ran in little streams down its flanks.

She rode into a small draw that had a good hill on both sides. Fog had settled in patches along the top of the bank on the opposite side. A herd of elk that had been in the bottom of the draw spooked and ran up the distant bank on the other side. Their tracks cut through the snow and exposed the grass in their path. Lacey stopped to look. She had only seen elk one other time in her life. The herd had a number of cows and calves in it and was being followed by a large bull. The bull was just getting his horns and stubs the size of a pick handle protruded from his head on either side. They were about four-teen inches long.

Lacey waited until the herd disappeared into a little island of trees that the fog had settled on. The last one to go was a young calf from the year before. He stopped and watched the buggy from a spot just at the top of the trees. She heard the lead cow bark and the calf tossed his head and trotted out of sight.

It was cold, but she was glad she had come. It was proof to her that there was a life waiting that she would have never known any other way. She lifted the reins and dropped them onto the rump of the mare. Water shook off the reins as she did and dripped onto the horse's rump.

The road was open. It was muddy and the little buggy slid down into the ruts and slopped back and forth as she went. She was following the wagon road that the stage took. The stage was someplace out ahead of her. She didn't have a map to Bozeman but she planned to stay on the stage route and get direc-tions as she went.

By the end of that first day, the snow had mostly melted again and the wind had slowed down to a chilly little breeze. She was chilled to the bone and the stage stop she landed at was a welcome sight.

She stabled her horses, took her bag and went inside. At first, no one seemed to notice her. People came and went all the time.

The first to realize she was a woman was the waiter who took her order at the table where she sat. He literally took a step back when she looked up at him. The road was not so dangerous as to fear traveling alone, especially for short distances, but a woman alone and so far from any town could be unwise, especially if the woman was planning to see a lot of open country where help would be hard to find if she needed it. It was not something often done by single women. They usually took the stage. These days they could even take a train if they found one going their way.

Lacey wasn't sure where she might end up so she stuck with the shiny new buggy.

The waiter was surprised to see her. Through the window he saw the buggy come in and was expecting a man. The little shop had four tables, and with Lacey they were all full from the stage that had just arrived in front of her. So for her sake, the waiter thought it best not to speak loud enough to be noticed.

He was a young man, and she assumed he must be the son of the people who owned the stage stop. He had on a white apron and denim jeans. Under the apron was a linen shirt. He was a rather tall man with a big smile and a full beard. He had his hair parted in the middle and combed down on both sides.

He leaned over close to Lacey's face and almost whispered in her ear. "Is it safe for you to be out here all alone?" He wanted to know.

Lacey was taken back a little. Why did he care? Was he really interested in her safety or was he testing her metal? The last thing she wanted was to have someone like this guy using his master key to open her door in the middle of the night. She had left home prepared for things like this and she was glad she did.

He was way too close to her face for comfort, like he was using privacy for a Trojan horse to get as close as he could. Lacey slipped her hand down the front of her culottes to the garter around her upper thigh. The waiter watched in shock at what she appeared to be doing.

In truth, he had frightened her a little and brought home the fact that she was at least to some degree vulnerable. When she pulled her hand out of her culottes she was holding a double barrel derringer. She pointed it straight at his face.

"I think so," she whispered back. "Do you people still sell coffee around here?"

The waiter's eyes widened like he had just noticed a coiled rattlesnake in her lap. He stepped back a little but kept his eyes on Lacey's lap. He tried to smile but all he could muster was a sort of grin. "Yes ma'am," he said, and hurried off to the other side of the room.

Lacey put the little shooter back in its silk-lined scabbard while she waited. *I guess that wasn't really all that ladylike,* she told herself. *But if he don't like the heat maybe he should stay out of the kitchen.* She could have managed with a smile and he would have fallen all over himself to help her. But she liked the power the little pistol gave her. It made her feel a lot more independent. Janice, in spite of herself, had given her the little weapon for a parting gift on the day that she left.

"Some men like to play rough," she told her. "It's best if they know who they are playing with."

It was a nice thing to do, like a thing between grown women. She never knew her mother felt that way about her. It made her feel good. It was a good gift. More than just a gift it was a statement. One she would never forget. All her life she had practiced her survival technique on men, and she usually got the result she expected. In a way, it gave her the idea that all she needed was her best smile and a little flirt to open the doors she meant to pass through.

But things were different now. Now she would need something more, something like the little pistol. It worked like the whip and chair thing the lion tamer at the traveling circus used. The other way had always worked, especially with Ed, but there was one who it didn't seem to have any effect on at all. That was the one she was following. Talon Windcatcher.

Perhaps that was what Talon had done that she found so attractive. He was a nice guy, but he was hard as flint when it came to the famous Lacey smile.

Her long blond hair and bright blue eyes were how she normally pulled it off. All the other men she knew were pretty much at her beck and call. Talon just smiled and went back to what he was doing. It was a new thing, and not one she liked. Yet, in another way, it drew her to him. He seemed more man than she was able to conquer. That part she liked, it made her feel more like a woman.

She had no idea what she would do when she caught up with him. He wouldn't take her with him in the first place, but maybe now that she was older he might. If not, she told herself, he would still be stuck with her. Where else do I have to be? At least Talon is my friend.

The waiter was a good test run. She was cold, tired, and hungry. She didn't feel like making any new friends, especially pushy ones.

The next day was a lot nicer day. The horses were fresh, and the road was all but dry by noon. She had lost sight of the stage while taking care of her horses. Her buggy was a lot lighter than the stage but the stage had four Morgans pulling it. Even so, the speed they traveled seemed to her a break-neck pace that should kill a normal horse. She held back and let the sun stand warm on her buggy and horses. It felt good.

The land had a little less grass this day and more pine and brush. The sky was blue and clear and she saw antelope and deer on occasion. The road passed large rock that had green, and sometimes red, lichen on it where cottontail rabbits like to hang out, and she noticed a rock chuck on the road at one spot where a small cool stream crossed the road over tiny pieces of brown and reddish colored rock. The water was clear and cool. She stopped at the little stream to drink and water the horses and moved on.

For the rest of her trip to Bozeman, she held her course. She followed the stage and got to each stop just after it did or at least not long after. She didn't worry that much about trouble with highwaymen or the like.

Getting closer to Bozeman did cause her a little worry. In her bag was a lot of money Ed had given her in cash. She wanted to put it in a bank account and just take a cashier's check but didn't want to take the time at Wolf Creek. She was at the bank with Ed and Janice on the day they split the money but she couldn't let her mother know she had been given more in cash. She worried about that now and planned to do it in Bozeman.

She didn't really trust a check, but the rest of the money was in check form anyway. Now she wondered if they would not question her for having so much cash and worry about doing business with her. She had a signed note from Ed but that alone was about good for nothing. She could have gotten something like that anywhere.

The city of Bozeman was a lot bigger than she first realized and she got a little turned around for a while. It wasn't so big that it was all that confusing to her, and in a couple hours, she had a pretty good handle on the lay of things. She found a bank that would do the business she needed, and they told her where the office for the sheriff was. The next day found Lacey on the road to Cougar Rock.

CHAPTER 9
I'm Home, Dear

Larry Adams was standing on the boardwalk on the main street in front of the blacksmith shop doing nothing, while he waited for the stage that would take him out of Cougar Rock for good, when Lacey rode into town. She was looking for Domingo Wells first and foremost.

The first person she saw was Larry. He was as burnt out with Cougar Rock as he was with the hotel he had just boarded up and put up for sale. It had once been a good business but the last two years had not gone well, and then came the fire. He threw his hands up and just wanted out while he still had a buck or two in the bank.

Lacey pulled up close enough to call over to him. "Hate to be a bother," she said, "but could you tell me where I might find Sheriff Wells?"

"The sheriff," Larry said," that's easy. He ain't been here long enough to find good places to hide yet. Just go on down the street to his office on the same side we are."

Larry was out of time. The stage he had been waiting for had just passed by right before Lacey pulled in. He needed to get to the store where he could get his things loaded. But being a business-man, he couldn't pass the off chance to sell the hotel. It was a long shot. He had already tried to sell it to Louis with no luck, and she was someone he had never seen before.

"You ain't interested in a great business here about are you?" He asked. "I'm selling the hotel, right where it stands, how it stands."

"No thanks," said Lacey. She was headed out as

soon as she was able to learn what direction she was headed.

Larry tipped his hat and started for the stage. Lacey looked over at the man in the blacksmith shop. He had walked out from inside and was standing under the sign that hung by chains on either end. The sign had the words on it "THE ANVIL". He was the smithy and he was smiling at her. He had a rag in his hand and was rubbing something he had just finished cooling in the dip tank. She smiled back and politely waved, then she flipped her reins and headed for the sheriff's office.

Domingo was at his desk when she tied up out in front. She decided she would see Domingo first, and eat later. Maybe even stay a day or so to wait for the next stage, if she needed to keep going. Domingo had given her the slip twice already, and this time if he was here she had him pinned down, but she wasn't taking anything for granted. The stage had just pulled up at the general store and was loading and unloading. She noticed Larry hustle up the boardwalk and disappear behind the stage.

She stepped down from her buggy and walked in through the open door of the sheriff's office. Someone was pounding nails into the wall outside, nailing up board and batten siding.

It was good to see that the man at the desk was in fact, Domingo.

"Good morning Sheriff," said Lacey.

Domingo looked up from a WANTED poster he had just gotten from the bigger Bear Valley. He was looking for one that might match the dead man. He had never seen the man, but if he found something, someone who had would know.

At first, he wasn't sure who he was looking at, but giving her a closer look he realized who she was. "Lacey Clanton!" Domingo said. He could hardly believe his eyes. "You're a long way from home."

"Depends on where you call home," Lacey said. "I'm looking for the Indian you chased out of Wolf Creek a few years ago. When I find him I'll be home."

Domingo wasn't sure what all that meant, but he

did know who she was talking about. "You mean Talon Windcatcher. He lives about five miles from here. I can tell you…"

He never got to finish the sentence. Lacey turned and ran out of his office at a fast trot. Domingo batted his eyes and watched her start across the street. She was moving like she had just spotted her face on one of the WANTED posters. Half-way across the street, her old hat blew off and she stopped, turned to pick it up and then changed her mind and left it there.

She rounded the stage, just as the passengers were loading. Larry was at the end of the line. She was out of breath, and she was also out of time. She ran straight up to Larry and looked him in the eyes. She suddenly realized she had no name to address so she flung out her hand to shake and said.

"Hi, I'm Lacey Clanton, we need to talk."

Larry was a little stunned. But he remembered her from a few minutes ago at the Anvil. At first, he was not sure what to say.

"Look, I have some money," she said. "If I like your deal, you can leave here a richer man."

Larry gathered his thoughts and realized he might have sold the hotel. "You up there," he called to the man loading the bags onto the top of the stage. "Changed my mind, I'll catch the next stage leaving town. Toss down my bags, could ya?"

That was the day Lacey made good on her promise to Talon. It was the day she moved into Cougar Rock. The hotel wasn't much, but it was a start. Larry showed her around. The fire damage he showed her from outside and assured her that the repairs would be easy enough. He told her of some of the men in town who might be willing to stop mining long enough to help out. If they were not finding much gold, they would work for a little while for another stake.

The hotel had been built into the side of the hill so that the top of it was only a few feet over the ridge of the hill. A windmill pumped up cold water that was held in a wood tank on the top of the ridge caused by the hill. It allowed for gravity to pull the water down into the rooms for running water.

The idea was good, but the work was not so good. The pipe was poorly insulated in places and froze all the time. There were enough threaded unions in it to supply a hardware store, from all the times it had been repaired. Some of the rooms had been flooded from broken pipes when the renters let the room fire get low enough to freeze the pipes inside. None of the piping inside had ever been insulated in the first place.

Lacey made a good deal on the place because of all the failings. She knew she would have her hands full getting it all worked out, but it really didn't look all that bad to her. Had she known what she was looking at, she might not of thought so, but she had accomplished one of the things she knew she wanted. She was home. The rest she would work out later.

New innovations were needed, but she still had a good deal of money. Overall, it looked like the perfect thing. The more she thought about it, the more she felt excited about it. She had landed in the same place Talon was and she had a way to feed herself. The world was looking a lot brighter. As soon as Larry was paid off, Lacey returned to Domingo's office.

"Sorry to run out on you this morning," she said. "I had pressing business to attend to."

"Hope you got what you went looking for," said Domingo. He wanted to ask what the hurry was, but more than that he wanted to know what she was doing in Cougar Rock.

Domingo leaned back in his chair until it rested against the wall. He was looking at Lacey. "You're quite a surprise," he said. "You come all this way alone?"

"I did," said Lacey. "I said I would, and I did."

"Yes you did," Domingo said. "Mind if I ask why?"

"Well, where else would I go? The ranch was sold, Dad went his way, Mom went hers, and I went mine."

Domingo thought on it for a little and decided to go on. "You know, not to spoil anything for you, but you know Talon has a wife now and a child."

Lacey wasn't one to let anyone under her skin. She had no way of knowing Talon would be married. In fact, she had thought very little about it. It was more of a let down than she was willing to let on about. "Good for him," she said. "That has nothing to do with my business. I wanted to be where I knew someone to get started. Talon was the only one I knew that I call a friend. You don't regret that I came, do you, Sheriff?"

The question seemed odd to Domingo. "Of course not," he said. "What town would not want a pretty young woman living in it. You are planning to stay I assume."

"I should hope so," she said, "I just bought the West Branch Hotel. Is there a place I can stay until I can get it up and running again? I think I want to make a cafe in the bottom of it."

"Well," said Domingo, "I'm pretty new here myself. All I can tell you is that your new investment is under a little investigation due to the fire. We might be coming in and out a little and sometimes might show up where you don't expect us to be. We'll try to stay out of your way though."

"Investigation?" Lacey said. "Mr. Adams never mentioned that."

"Well," said Domingo, "We think that the fire was maybe arson. It could also be connected to a killing here in town. He probably never mentioned that either."

"No," she said, "he certainly didn't."

Lacey let the news of the legal matters soak in for a little before she went on. "What does this mean for me?" She asked, "Will I still be able to do my repairs, or am I stopped until you're finished?" She was getting madder by the minute. She even thought about trying to get at least some of her money back. The deal might not be as sweet as she thought it was.

"Well," said Domingo, "I won't stop you from making repairs, but I will be underfoot for a while and if you find anything suspicious around the place you need to let me know."

That was a big relief. For a moment she thought

she had bought into something that might take years to clear.

"As far as a place to stay," said Domingo, "you now own the only place in town. But some of the rooms are still good. Shouldn't be a problem. The only place to eat now is the saloon. They have a few tables on the side away from the bar, but I warn you the food is less than you might have become used to. It will be a pleasure having an actual cook in town if you can salvage the place."

The fire was not that big a deal to her at the moment. It would pass. The news about Talon was somewhat bigger. The thought of him being married had never crossed her mind. She had always thought of him the way he was. When she thought about it, she realized that it had been almost four years since she last saw him. Anything could happen in four years. He could have been killed in that time.

The dream that drove her had a time lock of sorts. Thinking on it, she realized how silly that was. They were young. Her life was always about the same, so she just never thought about things being different. It seemed silly when she brought it to reason. Still, it would be good to see him again, and she had to start someplace.

Being near Talon was a better place than any other she could think of. The last she knew he was her friend and that alone was worth it. The rest would take some getting used to. It was a letdown but certainly not insurmountable.

Lacey left the sheriff's office and walked back across the street and up to the hotel. She unloaded her buggy and stowed her things in the lobby. She looked around again. Grey soot and smoke stain covered everything to some degree. That, she decided would be her first challenge. The mess left by years of misuse covered in smoke. It didn't smell as bad as she expected. At least that was something.

When she had finished sweeping a place off on one of the tables, she dropped her stuff on it and set out. She needed to leave her horses and buggy at the stable and find something to eat.

She was about to leave the lobby when she noticed her image in the mirror over the fireplace mantel. She almost laughed out loud. She really did look more like a man than a woman. She checked the pitcher pump in the cooking area of the hotel lobby and found water. It was cold but she didn't want to take time to start a fire to warm it. She washed up, changed clothes, and then she did something she had wanted to do ever since she left home. She brushed out her hair and left it down to drift in the wind.

"This one's for you Mom," she said out loud.

It looked like she was going to have to check out her competition. She also thought she might want another shot at Larry Adams. She felt like he had played her a little. She decided she wanted to ask for some of her money back. It turned out that the investigation didn't really change anything, but had she known, she might have asked for a better deal because of it.

She chose a light green dress that went down to her ankles and lace-up boots with somewhat high heels. The boots were black and polished to a nice shine. They drew attention to her as she walked down the boardwalk in front of the stable where she left her horses and buggy.

Louis Willis watched her cross the street after she left the stable. He knew from the buggy who she was, but he might not have recognized her otherwise. He watched until she entered the saloon and then went back to work.

Once across the street, Lacey stopped to look around before she went into the saloon. She was glad she did; the old dog she had noticed when she arrived was right where he had been when she first saw him. The street was full of people coming and going and miners were everywhere. She wondered if she should have a chaperone to go inside but she had no idea who it might be. She turned to go in when her eye caught a man riding a bay horse with a pack horse behind him. What made him noticeable was what he was packing on the pack horse. It was the bags she had helped him carry to the hotel.

Larry Adams had decided not to wait for the stage. He was leaving town as she watched and had already started around the large ponderosa before she noticed him. She thought of trying to call him back but decided to let it go. She went on into the saloon and found a table as near to the door as possible.

CHAPTER 10

PRYING EYES

Aggie was about to collect the evening dishes when she remembered something she had forgotten to talk to Talon about. Talon and Reed were still seated at the table, so she sat down at her place again.

"Talon," she said, "is there any way we can stop people from coming too close to the cabin on the other side of the Ox Bow?"

"Well it's not our land," said Talon, "but why would you want to?"

"Might be nothing," she said, "but there has been a man there on two separate days now. He don't look like other miners. He has a black vest and hat and he never looks dirty like he should. He seems to spend a lot of time watching the house. If he sees me notice him he quickly goes back to his pan. But I don't think he is what he wants me to think he is. It bothered me enough to bring Reed in from the balcony. I think he watches him also."

Talon felt the blood rush to the top of his head. He had never had a reason to worry for his family before. It was a somewhat helpless feeling. He had to work and couldn't always be home. If someone was watching the house, that might have to change. He needed to deal with that first. Whoever it was, if they were up to something, had to know how to stay out of sight of the barn across the street and they knew his normal schedule.

"How long has this been going on?" Talon asked.

"Well," said Aggie, "he wasn't there today but he has been for the last two days before that. He wandered up the bank as far as the mountain would let him, and looked around there and then went back to the place on the bank where he was working.

I didn't want to say anything, but today I saw him on the other side of the Clearwater. He waved like we were old friends or something. You were in the back property someplace. I came back inside. I get a bad feeling about him. He seems creepy to me. We don't know him, why would he do that? Do you think it could be the one who left the tracks in the cave?"

"Could be," said Talon. He thought about what he had just heard and decided Aggie had been right about a dog. In fact, he wondered why he hadn't found one a long time ago.

"Tomorrow," said Talon, "I want to go into town. I want to take you and Reed with me. We will make a day of it. We need to get up early and hit the road. I want to get over onto the reservation and see Tony about a dog. I also want to see Joseph Long about a gun. I want one I can carry on my hip. In fact, I might want one you can keep handy here at home too."

Talon and Aggie left before daylight and headed for town first. He wished he could have used the back trail to the old crossing in case anyone was watching the house and would know that they had left, but the wagon was too wide for the trail.

They arrived in town too early for the general store to be open. In fact, the town was not moving at all yet. Axle Ford, however, was out and sitting on a chair leaned back against the wall in front of the saloon waiting for it to open so he could get breakfast.

Domingo was right about the food, but he hated his own even worse and the city paid for his meals as part of his pay. He was glad Lacey meant to start a cafe in the old hotel. Even the coffee was burnt at the saloon. He waved as he watched Talon's wagon go by.

A road had been built to the Reservation and it cut the travel time in half to go there. It was around eleven in the morning when Talon reached Tony's cabin. Tony Blackhawk met him in the front yard.

"You brought your family," he said happily. "Will is going to love that."

Will was Tony's son. His full name was Willow, but most of the time he was called just Will. He came out of the cabin behind his father and stood beside him scratching his fat little bare belly. He had on a pair of red wool pants and a black shirt that hung open in the front. It had buttons, but Tony and his wife Black Doe had given up on making him button it up. He was still learning to keep his clothes on at all, and they were grateful for what they had been able to talk him into.

His small round belly protruded slightly from the front of the shirt. The sun had darkened his skin to an even brown. He looked happy. He smiled when he saw Reed. They had met a few times before when Talon came to get horses.

"You need horses?" Tony wanted to know.

"Not today," said Talon. He let Reed down while Aggie stepped down and went in to talk to Black Doe. "Today I need a dog."

The two boys had already disappeared around the corner of the cabin and were gone from sight.

"No dogs here," said Tony. "Puppies though."

Talon didn't like the sound of a puppy but he was willing to take what he could get. *It'll grow,* he told himself. "What kind of puppies?" he wanted to know.

Something tugged at his pants loop and he looked down. It was Reed. He had a six-or-so week old puppy in his arms. He looked up at Talon with a big smile. Will was with him; he had one under each arm. They looked like Border Collie pups. They were all black except for a white collar and a white blaze down their faces. Both the boys were smiling up at him. No words could have said it clearer. Talon had a dog.

"Never mind," said Talon, "looks like we already have a puppy." Tony laughed.

"You can buy two if you want," he said.

Talon smiled down at Reed. "One'll do."

After visiting a while, Talon and Aggie started

back for Cougar Rock. Reed sat in the wagon box now. He had seen enough scenery. The puppy was in his lap, and now and then he laughed at it when it wanted to play. He had a small piece of rope they were playing tug-o-war with.

Talon got back to town right before the store closed, and found what he needed on the rack behind the counter. He bought a twelve gauge for the house and a Smith and Wesson Thirty-eight with a hip holster. He knew they would need a lot of practice with both guns, so he bought a lot of ammunition while he was there. He hoped he would never have to shoot anyone, but if it came to that he wanted to be one split second faster, and a tiny bit better than the man he was needing to kill.

Axle Ford was busy working the case of the dead man. He made a visit to the gravel bar where the body was found. The gravel bar extended out from the bank not far from town. No one was there when he arrived. The sun was bright and the water clear and clean. That was becoming a rare thing. Usually, there was at least some mud in it from the mining. Most of that work had moved up to the headwaters now, and the river had time to clear before it got to town.

The rocks were clean and warm. Grass grew along the shore, but the spring flow had stripped the bar clean of vegetation earlier in the year. A few pines held tenaciously to the edge of the bank and dead wood lay in the pine needles under them. He looked around in the path that led out to the bar and spooked a seagull off a rock near the water's edge as he entered the open bar.

It was a nice day to be out. The sound of the fast water was soothing and made the air feel cool and good. He began his search on the upstream end. He had learned that the body had been found near the trail that led down to the bar but he didn't want to miss anything that might be related. He searched the bar to the point of even turning over rocks looking for anything that might be a clue.

The dead man had not been robbed. That haunted him. If there had been a fight that got out of hand there should be some sign of it in the sand and gravel. There were man tracks that had occurred since the shooting but no scuff marks or any blood splatter on the rocks. A fight would most likely have involved blood. And a shooting always did. He wondered if the body had been dumped there.

Another thing that bothered him was the camp. Where was the dead man's camp? If he was a miner he would have a camp. Axle had been upriver and down and had talked to a lot of people. This guy was rarely seen and the only people who had ever talked to him were the people he sold insurance to.

The bar produced nothing, so his next stop was Dennis Caldwell. He owned the stable and had bought insurance from the guy. It was odd to him that nobody had remembered the man's name. And the only paperwork they had been given was a form showing that they were insured.

Small town people were more gullible than he could imagine. They all paid in cash. The contracts were good for one year from the date of purchase. *Must have been a smooth talker*, thought Axle.

Dennis had one of the contracts. He had paid fifty dollars for insurance on the stable for one year. It was to protect against flood and fire, and even some vandalism. That seemed like a good enough deal. The problem was that he paid cash and the receipt was handwritten and signed Douglas Brogan Broker on the bottom.

At last, he had a name for the corpse, even if it was not his real name. The name of the supposed insurance company was Handover Insurance. There was no contact information on the receipt or the contract. Axle shook his head and started out for the sheriff's office with Dennis's paperwork in hand.

CHAPTER 11
IT'S A SMALL WORLD

Lacey had combed every inch of the hotel getting to know the layout. She hated the old jail but wasn't sure what to do about it. Workers were everywhere she looked and she started feeling like she was getting in the way. She decided to go down to the saloon and trading post and take a break.

Joseph Long saw her walking past the store and called out to her. He had been doing a little shopping and searching catalogs he had recently gotten in the mail. In one of the catalogs was a pressurized water system with a pump that could supply an entire hotel. Lacey liked the idea and he ordered her one. It would pump water through a pipe under the street from the river. Well insulated, it would make her whole business much better, especially the kitchen. She left the store in a good mood, and started down the boardwalk.

The street was always a busy place. She liked that it was so different from Ed's little ranch. Dust lifted and drifted by with the wagons and people as they went their way. The warm sun shone against their faces and reflected bright off bit rings and buckles.

Now and then she noticed someone watching her as they passed. She liked that too. She liked wearing her hair down. It was almost like a statement. Her mother had said that it was a "come on" to men and hated her doing it. As far as Lacey could tell, that was mostly because her mother didn't like the competition. It moved in the wind and felt good, but it collected dust so badly that she usually had it lifted and tied at the back of her head.

A man she had never seen before trotted by on a tall black horse. He had two blue-looking dogs that stayed on his heels. The man was wearing blue jeans and a black shirt. He had a well-blocked black hat and sat up straight in the saddle. It made him look tall. He was a narrow-faced man with a beard. He smiled at Lacey so she smiled back and turned her head away politely.

Lacey was dressed for work in a long gray dress and she had a ladies' hat she grabbed on her way out. Her boots announced her coming as she stepped lightheartedly down the boardwalk. She didn't bother slowing down when she stepped off the boardwalk onto King Street.

The man on the tall horse turned in front of her to go down King Street and she waited for him to pass. When he did her heart stopped cold. Leaning against a lamppost on the other side of King Street was a tall blond man dressed in a black leather vest. He had black pants and a worn shirt.

It was the shirt she recognized first. Her mother

had made it for one of her lovers who she had visited anytime she could in Wolf Creek. She had also seen him on Ed's ranch when Ed was out working. He was one that Lacey knew well. Jeffery Baker was staring straight at her. She stopped in the street and thought about going back to the hotel but knew he would only follow her.

Cougar Rock just became a lot darker. If there was one man in the world she never wanted to see again it would be Jeff. She hated him for who he was. And she knew what he was, an underhanded cheat and a user.

He always had the same smile on his face. It gave him a sort of dominance, like he had you right where he wanted you. How he found his way to Cougar Rock she couldn't guess. She hoped he hadn't somehow followed her. That was thought for some other time. Right now all she wanted was to get shed of him and never see him again.

There was nothing else she could do. The last thing she wanted to do was make it look like she was running from him. She decided to go on to the saloon in spite of him. As she stomped by, Jeffrey tried to grab her arm but she pulled free and turned red-faced back in the direction of the saloon.

"Hold on there," he said, "just trying to say Hi. Never dreamed I would find 'you' here."

Lacey was way ahead of him. She knew Jeff well enough to know that she was the only one surprised. He no doubt planned things more or less this way.

By now he would have already been sure of where she was living and what she was doing. He was a sneak but he was a sneak who knew how to be the hunter or the hunted. Whatever he wanted, he had a plan on how to get it and somehow she played into the plan.

She ignored what he said and hurried on down the street and into the saloon. There were people at all but one table and more coming in and out in a somewhat constant flow. The one table that was available was almost in the center of the room. It was a small table with two chairs. She chose the one on the back of the table so she could see the door.

Jeff had already entered before she even sat down. He went straight to the table where she was. Without asking, he pulled out the chair that remained and took a seat.

"I know you don't like me much, Lacey," he said, "but just listen for a minute. All I want is to let the past be the past. We got a whole new life here, you and me. This ain't no way to treat each other after all we been through."

She wasn't sure what he meant by all they had been through. All she knew was that he used her mother, made a fool of Ed, who was the only father she ever knew, and treated her like a red-headed stepchild. When she was younger, if he came around, he was fond of putting his hands where she didn't like. He made her feel vulnerable when she was a child.

"I don't care what you think we have been through, Jeff. I don't like you and I don't want you anywhere near me. And if you don't leave, I'm going to start screaming and get you thrown in jail." Just for a moment she thought of the old jail in the hotel and wished they had not built the new one.

"Listen Lacey," he said, "you start screaming and both us are going to look bad. I wouldn't mind telling the whole world about us. In fact, I would like to. So if that's what you want, then start screaming, but at least hear me out first. All I need is a little help, then if you want I will go and you won't see me again. I can't get that help any other place I know of. I just need a little information that you can get for me."

Lacey could feel her face getting red. She had no idea what he wanted, and she didn't care. What she did know was that she had no intention of getting involved with Jeff Baker.

"Help you?" Lacey spat. "I wouldn't throw you a stretch of barbed wire if you were drowning in my outhouse hole. Why do you think I would want to help you? I hate you."

135

Jeff could feel the blood turning his face red. He was going to need another angle. He had dealt with Lacey's mother long enough to know that she was going to need a little push. Mr. nice guy needed to take a back seat. His features hardened, and his eyes grew cold.

"I'll tell you why," said Jeff. He had a dark look on his face it made him look violent and angry. "Because if you don't, I can ruin you in this little town and your Indian friend will go down with you. All I got to do is start talking bout how well you and him got to know each other on Ed's little ranch when you were a little younger."

There was no doubt in Lacey's mind what he was implying. She was innocent, but she wished she wasn't. In any case, he was right. It would ruin her, and it would ruin Talon as well. The threat made her feel trapped and helpless, but only for a moment. She needed time, and she knew how to get some. She stood up fast and let her rage take control. The instant the idea came to her, she knew what she wanted to do. In fact, she realized she had wanted to do it for as far back as she could remember. He had been the wedge in her family's home for most of her entire life. This was a long time coming and she didn't care what happened after.

Her hand came from someplace behind her. It was traveling about the speed of light when it found Jeff's face. She wanted to punch him, but she wasn't sure she knew how, so she slapped him with all her might. Jeff never saw it coming. Snot and saliva flew across the room and he had to catch himself from falling out of the chair. His head jerked out from under his hat quick enough that the hat hit the floor beside the chair.

Before Jeff realized what had happened, the entire place had fallen silent. The slap had sounded like a small arms weapon going off in the room and every eye was on them. The old dog had slipped in to escape the heat and was lying on the floor by the back wall. The sound sent him clawing his way outside in a panic.

Jeff was instantly infuriated and embarrassed. What he wanted to do was punch her in the face, but he knew he couldn't. So did Lacey. She was still standing. He stood up like someone ready to do something and in that moment he might have. He was glaring at Lacey.

She had seen that look before. Right before he had slapped her mother in past times. Today the time and place had been perfect. There was nothing he could do. She knew that at least for the moment she was the one in control. She was pretty sure she had the upper hand in another way as well, He seemed like he really did need her help.

He was at a loss for what to do. He wanted to hit her back. Had she not been in public he would have, even knowing that it might only make her more resistant to helping him. For the moment he was at her mercy, and thought about sitting down again. The thought lasted just long enough to realize that the wall behind her seemed to move. It caught his attention. He looked over her shoulder to see what had just happened. The wall turned out to be Louis Willis. He had watched Lacey enter the saloon from his shop across the street. When she was inside he followed her.

Ever since he first laid eyes on her he had been watching for her. She was like the last perfect rose on a dying vine to him. One very beautiful thing who appeared to be in the world all by herself, and he wanted to get to know her a lot better before someone else did. The problem was that he was shy of women and had no good way to get her attention.

Jeff had just solved that problem for him. He was just a little shorter than Jeff but almost twice his width. Muscles bulged out from under his shirt as he stood up. Every nerve in his body came alert and the veins in his neck stood out over the heavy muscle that ran high off his shoulder. He was big as a bull and ready to charge. He really wanted Jeff to try something, and Jeff could see he did. Jeff could also see that he had no chance of surviving the fight if one broke out.

Louis was standing six feet behind Lacey staring at Jeff. He had stood at the same time as Jeff and he was staring at him with the look of a man who was enjoying the moment. Jeff decided the moment was over. His face was red and Lacey's handprint was visible even through his beard. He was whipped and he knew it. He bent down, picked up his hat, and strutted out of the saloon.

CHAPTER 12

THE WRITING ON THE WALL

Lacey stood for a moment watching Jeff leave the saloon. A few seconds after the door swung closed, the people began talking again. At first in hushed tones and then as the room regained its energy, it began to sound normal as before. She was embarrassed and she knew that her face must be red but she was also elated. She knew she had not heard the last of Jeff. In fact, she was certain he would try to get even. But for now, she felt like a prize-fighter on a winning night.

The faces turned away and Lacey began to worry. She knew she had to leave sooner or later and she was sure Jeff would also know. She was loving the look on his face in her mind when the picture in her mind made her realize that he wasn't looking at her. He was looking over her shoulder and whatever he saw had sent him packing.

She turned to see what it was he had been looking at. Louis was still standing. He smiled his best nice-guy smile and held out his hand. His shirt was a sleeveless Johnny top and he had on denim coveralls that showed the day's work. It was his smile that she liked.

"Hi," he said, "I'm Louis Willis."

Lacey took his hand in hers and shook it gently. "So you are," she said. She remembered him from the Anvil. Now she knew his name. He was a welcome sight. "I'm Lacey Clanton. Pleased to meet you, Louis."

She was suddenly feeling a lot safer. Her eyes followed his powerful body from his boots up to his disheveled light brown hair. He had taken off his hat and was holding it at chest level. He looked like a good man to have for a friend. The eager look on his face made her smile. She had seen "that" look before.

"Friend of yours?" Louis asked.

"No, but I can't deny that I know him. You wouldn't mind walking me back to the hotel would you?"

As she might have assumed, he would have paid good money to walk her back to the hotel. Louis was a lonely man. He didn't like the easy women in the saloon and he hadn't seen anyone else he did like, that wasn't married or too young.

He worried that he was being a little too obvious but he couldn't help himself. She wasn't just a potential mate; she was a lot better looking than he might have hoped for. Having the Anvil gave him a little confidence that she might be interested in him if she was interested in men at all, and now she might actually need him.

They left the saloon together and started down the street arm in arm. Louis made her feel like a kept women. Lacey made him feel like a million bucks. He stood tall and proud and tried to walk as slow as he could without being too obvious.

Across the street from inside the stable, Jeff watched them until he could no longer see them in the throng of people that filled the dusty streets of Cougar Rock. The day was leaning toward evening and the heat was starting to wane as Jeff left the stable. He was disappointed but not defeated. He had a lot invested and wasn't planning on giving up anytime soon.

His face wasn't even losing the fingerprints of Lacey's hand yet, and he was already planning his next move. He started down the dirt street edge along the corral for the stable. He was deep in thought and soon stopped to lean against a corral pole.

He rolled a cigarette, lit it with a stick match, and watched it burn down in his fingers. The sun was low in the sky and the wind was moving slowly up the river. A chipmunk popped out from under the wooden stock tank the stable used to water horses. It sat for a moment and surveyed the corral and street and scurried away again when it noticed Jeff. It left a little dust cloud as it went that drifted up and disappeared down the street. Jeff watched it go and blew out the match. He tossed the remainder of the stick in the direction of the chipmunk and continued on his way.

A crow flew down off the roof of the saloon and lit on the street sign. It called out its familiar craw-craw, as if someone might be interested in the news and walked back and forth on the sign as it watched Jeff walk down Crossing Street towards the river.

Louis had questions. They were questions that he was wanting answers for, but he didn't feel confident enough to ask Lacey some things so soon. He decided to skip the "where are you from" ones and get to the closer-at-hand ones.

"Would it be pushy of me to ask who that guy was?" Louis asked.

Lacey wasn't in the mood to talk about Jeff. "He is an old thorn on a dead bush. Hopefully not one I will need to worry about."

"He seemed like he might be a threat," said Louis, "I wouldn't be intruding to offer my services would I?"

That made Lacey smile. She would have asked for his services if she needed to, but she was fairly certain he would offer. "No," said Lacey, "not at all. But you might miss a lot of work standing around waiting for something to happen." She wasn't that afraid of Jeff. He was a bully but he would cool off. Anyway, she believed him when he said that he needed her help. For the moment she was more interested in getting to know Louis than worrying about Jeff.

"Well, that's true," Louis said, "but I can make a lot of short visit trips for a while. That would be nice wouldn't it?"

He was looking at her eyes to try and read anything she might not say. She looked like a child with a new friend. Her happy smile was literally intoxicating. It made him smile back like they were sharing a secret that only they understood. Lacey leaned a little closer and said in a calming voice, "I think I would like that."

Lacey looked over her shoulder at the street behind them as they entered the hotel. There were a lot of people and she wasn't surprised that Jeff was no place in sight. She knew him well enough to know that if he had been there he would have made certain she knew it. It made her wonder where he was.

Construction was going well and the cafe was almost ready to open as they walked into the room. The back wall had been replaced and the plumbing was just getting finished. It was the new system Lacey had bought from the General Store.

Louis sat down at a new table Lacey had just added to the others.

"Coffee?" she offered.

"Sure," said Louis. "I would love some."

Lacey left for the kitchen in the next room while Louis waited. The tables already had menus on them.

There was also something there he had only seen in Bear Valley: napkin holders. Shiny metal ones with a lot of napkins in them. He was a little impressed.

The menus were standing in a little keeper fixed to the holders. Louis picked one up out of curiosity. It had a lot of things on it. Some of the things Lacey had learned from looking at the menus she saw on her trip to Cougar Rock. She had even started practicing some of the dishes for herself.

Some things he wasn't sure he even knew, but it all looked good. He turned the menu over in his hand and found that it had something written on the back. It read,

"Out of the root the rose bush grows, with thorns on its stem all the way to the rose."

It was an interesting thing to read on the back of a menu and he made a mental note to ask Lacey what it meant. He put the menu back in the holder. The hustle and noise of the construction echoed through the structure and now and then voices of workers could be heard talking.

Louis felt like he was watching his little town's history being built. He was hoping he was seeing his future being built with it.

Louis left the West Branch hotel three hours later and started down the street. He was certain that there would be people waiting for him at the Anvil and needing help, but work was somewhere way back on the back burner. As he walked down the boardwalk he began to whistle a little tune he didn't know he knew.

CHAPTER 13

LITTLE THINGS

Axle Ford made his living knowing the little things that others often overlook. He noticed a man's eyes and body language while he talked to him. A favorite pastime for him was to hang out in a saloon and listen and watch the people who came and went. A dark corner might serve his hobby for four or five hours at a time. He genuinely enjoyed doing it. Tonight he needed information and he set out to get it.

The sun had dropped below the peaks and dark was moving in. The shadow of the awnings over the boardwalks had reached the street, and the nightlife was about to begin as he slipped into the saloon and ordered a whiskey. He found his way to a corner table, pulled his hat down a little and started his wait.

Outside on the street, a half moon was just getting its night path figured out. It rose a little over the peaks and spot-lighted the main street of Cougar Rock. The night shadows began to grow out of nothing and stretched out as far as they could reach.

The night was warm and dry. The flies that haunted the day, and tormented both man and beast, were fading out for the night. Mosquitoes were fewer and stayed near any light source they could find, leaving the street mostly free of them.

It was the time of day that called to the lonely and restless. It was the time of day that Axle was waiting for, and he had not waited in vain. The saloon began to fill with people. He watched as the billiard table was set and made ready and the light over it turned on. Miners and locals gathered at the bar and one of the town drunks wandered in.

He looked like he had just woke up. His clothes were dirty and tattered and his hair was hanging in his eyes. It looked like it had not been washed since he was a kid. He was a short, stout man about five and a half feet tall. He had no hat. Axle wondered why a man would do that to himself. His whole life came down to finding enough money to get drunk one more time.

Nevertheless it was this very type of man he was looking for. They were the driving force of the evening. Loved or hated, they always stirred the pot. Often someone would say something to insult them and a conversation would start up, or someone would say something to another person in the presence of the drunk thinking it safe. They were often only about half conscious and forgot what they heard, if they even realized that they had heard it in the first place.

The table Axle chose was in the corner where

the drunk often sat and it forced him to move to another table a little closer to the crowd. Axle chose his table for that reason. He wanted to hear what the drunk was talking about before he got so plowed that he passed out.

If the drunk had a name, no one seemed to know it. They all just called him Jolly. He had striking blue eyes and long sandy hair. There was an old scar that crossed his eye and ran down his right cheek. His face was unshaven and dirty and looked like it had always been. He walked hunched over and Axle wondered if he was injured. His one leg seemed a little shorter than the other. He sat down hard at the table next to Axle's and leaned on one elbow while he nursed the double shot of whiskey he brought with him.

Axle sat in the shadow and waited. He too was sipping on whiskey. He waited for Jolly to finish and start looking around for a way to get more.

When he did Axle stretched out his leg far enough to bump the chair Jolly was setting in. It made him look around and Axle motioned for him to come sit for a little. He ordered another double for Jolly and had it set on the table. Jolly sat down at Axle's table and smiled as the whiskey was brought.

"How you been Jolly?" Axle asked, "Missed you last night."

Axle had not been in the saloon the night before but he wanted Jolly to think he looked forward to seeing him. It was a friendly gesture that a lonely person might be eager to accept.

"I been here," Jolly said, "ever night I been here."

"Must not have noticed," said Axle. "Here, have a shot on me."

Jolly had been keeping a close eye on the spare shot glass and smiled when Axle offered it to him. The saloon was full of people by that time and noisy. A billiard game had started and men surrounded the table to watch. Jolly was warming up to Axle and smiling a lot.

"How many these guys you know?" Axle asked him.

"Lots," said Jolly, "most all sometimes. Some nights not so many."

"Ever hear of a man selling insurance round here?" Axle watched Jolly's eyes as he spoke. He first looked confused like he wasn't sure, and then his eyebrows lifted a little.

"You mean the little guy, he was a fighter. Fast as a cat that guy. He could kick out your eyeball and bust your head before it hit the floor. Only came in a few weeks, ain't seen him now in a while."

"Fighter was he?" Axle said.

"Ya, pretty soon nobody wanted to fight im anymore." Jolly laughed and sipped his whiskey. "Not very big though, quiet too. Played pool good, and liked to gamble. Say what you spose happen to im?"

Axle leaned close to Jolly and spoke softly. He didn't want any nosy neighbors listening and he wanted Jolly to feel free to talk. "He have any friends, this little guy?" Asked Axle.

"Not here," said Jolly.

"Not here? Where then? Someplace else maybe?"

Jolly lifted his head to look at Axle. He looked a little concerned. His body straightened up a little like he was starting to wonder who Axle was and why all the questions. Axle waved to the barmaid. She was passing by a couple of tables over. He got another drink for Jolly.

"You was saying he had a friend someplace. That interests me, said Axle. Wish I could have met his friend and had a talk with the two of them. Might like to meet a fighter like that."

Jolly loosened up a little when he got the whiskey. "Ya, he liked to come here and he never brought his friend here. Only talked to him down by the river. I sleep in the stable sometimes. I seen em sometimes down at the river. His friend, he was a miner. Never saw him much, only way out on the island in the middle. Had a black hat, that guy. Kinda tall. They had no horses, those guys. Never see them on horses. Saw him way over on the river."

Jolly was getting a little drunker and losing his thoughts. Axle could see in his eyes that he had said all he was going to say, all that Axle wanted to hear anyway.

Axle had what he came for and he got it from the one guy in the room that does more listening and watching than talking. "You take care jolly," said Axle. He finished his drink in one shot and got up. He left half a dollar on the table for Jolly. Some friends are worth keeping, even if you keep them at arm's reach. That's the kind of friend he wanted in Jolly, a quiet one.

Morning found Axle on the braided islands of the river. From the stable, he studied the river and made note of all the little islands whose end he could see from there. It made the search a lot faster. The little islands were thick with underbrush and willow, and he was forced to follow trails that wandered through them, where he could find any. He moved from one island to the next and looked for more trails. By noon he found what he was looking for.

On the upstream tip of one of the larger islands, a little water had washed out a small, bare gravel passage. A small amount of water still trickled through it and a lot of digging had been done in it.

On the other side of the little wash, large willow trees and sagebrush blocked any view of the upper river, and inside the brush line under the heavy limbs of the willow, where the ground was bare, he found a small camp.

The fire had been an old one and the ashes were deep in the ring. The bed area was in soft sand tucked up under the willow so that it was not noticeable at first. The bedroll was still there. Mice and squirrels had been at it and chewed holes all over it, but otherwise, it looked like it had not been disturbed. The cooking utensils were hanging in the tree limbs and there was a saddle and tack on the ground.

The camp was old and well hidden. He was glad for that. No one had raided it yet. A magpie had been stealing bits of material from the bed for a nest. It stayed in the tree over the bed and squawked at him from just out of reach. Soon other magpies heard the news and began doing the same on other little islands.

Axle ignored the bird and went back to what he was doing. There was paper in the fire pit. It looked like a pile of paper had been burned there, so he carefully removed the ashes a little at a time until he had dug down to near the middle of what was once a small pile of stacked paper. Two pieces of paper were still partly intact. They were at least legible. They were copies of the insurance contracts like the ones Dennis Caldwell had received when he purchased his insurance. Some of them had been signed by the buyers. The rest were burned up.

He carefully stood up and looked around. The saddle was not chewed by rats, but the lining had been chewed a little on the edges. Bits of wool from it were on the ground around it. It looked like it had been dropped on the ground carelessly, the way someone might do in a hurry or drunk. He rolled the saddle over and looked under it. There wasn't anything there, but something did catch his eye when it flopped back down again.

On the other side of the saddle on the ground, there was a clean brass casing. It had dropped into a wild rose bush and lay on the ground under it. It was hidden in the willows and brush at the edge of the camp. If he had not been so close to the ground he could have easily missed it. It was about four feet into the camp from the entry on the little trail that led into it. He bent down and picked it up.

It was not like any casing he had ever seen before. It was short and stout looking. On the primer end, the caliber had been stamped. The casing belonged to a Smith and Wesson 35. Axle had never even heard of such a weapon. He sniffed the inside of the little cartridge. It was old. He knew he had found something and searched around for more of the little casings.

There were none, but something else just as important showed up in the sand around the bottom of the willows and wild roses across the camp from where he found the casing. There was old dried blood in the sand. It wasn't much but it was enough. He reasoned that it could be game blood of some kind, but he doubted it. It was also on the brush, and when he rolled a rock the size of a melon, there was a lot of blood on the underside.

What had been missing on the gravel bar where the body had been found was all over the place in the little hidden camp. He carefully folded the two remaining insurance contracts and put them into the saddlebags on the saddle and picked up the saddle. His horse was about a hundred feet from the camp and he set out to find it.

Axle took the findings and rode back into town. He went to the sheriff's office looking for Domingo. He found him coming back from the West Branch Hotel. It was open now and he went there for lunch. He waited in the open door of the office when he saw Domingo coming. The saddle was on the floor behind him. Domingo knew the look on Axle's face when he saw him.

"Well?" he said as he walked through the door.

Axle held out his open hand. He had the little empty cartridge in it. Domingo smiled and picked it up.

"And?"

"I found Brogan's camp," reported Axle. He told Domingo everything he had seen in the camp.

"Excellent," said Domingo. "We now have a kill site, and we might even have the gun that did it. What caliber is it?"

"35 Smith and Wesson," said Axle. "Ever heard of it?"

"Nope, maybe you should take it over to the store and see if Joseph Long can find it in one of his catalogs. If not, the trading post might know something."

Axle was reaching for the door when it opened in front of him. Jeff Baker walked in with a big smile.

"Mornin guys," he said, like he was talking to old friends. He was standing just inside the room. Axle knew the face but couldn't place him at first. Axle moved over to where Domingo was at his desk. As he walked, he tried to place the face and put a name to it.

Jeff was still waiting. He was a little surprised they didn't remember him right away. Domingo did, but he was surprised to see him. His mind began racing back to the last few days. That made him wonder all the more. "Well," he said, "if it ain't our old friend Jeffery Baker."

"So it is," Axle added. "Good to see you, Jeff. You just wandering, or you looking for more posse work?" The men all laughed a little at Axle's joke.

"Well, gold of course," said Jeff, "and thought it would be nice to see you guys again. Can't a guy just be stopping by to see old friends?"

"Well sure he can," said Domingo, "but you didn't come all the way to this little burg just looking for us did you?"

"Well no, not exactly," said Jeff. "I was working a little sand up on the headwaters and heard you was sheriff here. Thought I should stop by and see ya." He was still smiling and looking around. "See you got your self a nice new jail," he said. "Quiet little town and all must be a good place to work."

"We like it," said Domingo. "So, you got rich yet?"

Jeff laughed a little. "Not yet, but who can tell. I hear there is a good bit of gold around here. Laying right on top of the ground, they tell me. That is of course, if you are willing to listen to the local scuttlebutt, and if you're looking underground."

"You mean the caves," Domingo said. "Only heard of one story bout gold in a cave. You must be talkin bout the Windcatcher's cave. That old story sure is gettin around."

"Well," said Jeff, "don't reckon I know the name. I heard it was ol three feathers who had it. His real name is Windcatcher, is it? Well, that's interesting, you sound like it ain't true, the gold and all."

"Wouldn't know," said Domingo, "just heard the same stuff you did."

"Oh," said Jeff, "I was hoping you could tell me a little more about it, like where it is maybe."

The room fell silent for a moment while Domingo thought about what he believed Jeff might actually be looking for. "Don't know," he said, "been a lot going on round here. Haven't had time to run down any fables yet. Might be fun sometime though.

"On another point, you might be just the guy I need to talk to, you being a fine gun fancier and all. We found a strange casing down on the river. Never saw anything like it before. You might know a little about it. Show Jeff that little casing," Domingo said to Axle.

Axle handed Jeff the 35 Smith and Wesson casing. Jeff took the little casing and looked a little confused at it.

"Ever seen anything like that?" Domingo asked.

Jeff tipped the casing up and looked at the bottom of it. "35," he said. "That's interesting. This is the newest thing on the market for Smith and Wesson. Too small for most things, and danged expensive, but wouldn't mind having one. Where'd you find it?"

"Oh just laying around down on the river. Never owned one before I take it?"

"Nope." He handed the casing back to Axle. "Kinda surprised to see one, much less own one."

He put his hat back on and backed up one step towards the door. "You fellas take care. I'll stop by again when I get a little time. If you hear about that cave thing, be good to know."

"Keep you in mind," said Domingo. He tipped his chair back against the wall and watched Jeff leave the office. After the door shut, the two men sat in silence for a few seconds.

"So what's your take?" Domingo asked.

"He's lying," said Axle.

"Funny," said Domingo, "that was my take too. Might want to keep an eye on our old friend Jeff for a while. Where you spose he came from anyway? Doubt he just happened by."

"Don't believe he did," said Axle. "Ask me again in a week or so."

Chapter 14

Out of His Past

Long warm days passed by without much change. The restaurant and hotel had been open for a while, and people came and went like a dripping faucet.

Talon had managed to avoid town for a month or so and was glad to just be home. Aggie, however, not so much. She had a list and was running out of supplies. The trip to town was usually a once a month adventure and she looked forward to it like a small vacation.

Talon harnessed a team to the buckboard and drove it across the bridge to the house. After Aggie and Reed were loaded, he made sure that the doors were all locked. He double-checked the iron cave door.

As he left, he took a straw broom and cleared all the tracks that led to the porch and front door. The ground was left smooth and ready for any tracks that might happen in his absence.

He had installed a new gate on the house side of the bridge, and that he shut and slid the lock board into the notch in the corner post. After that, he walked to the wagon and pulled one of the tail hairs from one of the horses. He tied a knot in the hair at its end and slid the hair through a small split he had created with a knife. The other end of the hair he tied to a nail head that had been intentionally left up a little on the gatepost.

Any unaware intruder would slide the board back to open the gate and when the knot that had been snugged into the small split drew the hair tight it would break without them noticing. It wasn't designed to keep anyone out but keep him from

surprising anyone who might have made themselves at home while he was gone. If there was
someone in the house when he returned, he wanted
to know before he got to the porch and met a gun in
his face.

It was a nice ride to town. The road wandered
along the edge of the river and through brush and
pine. Small meadows of aspen groves came and
went where lupine and bluebells grew, and Indian
paintbrush grew along the edges of the road. Out on
one of the meadows, they spotted sage hens, and as
they rounded one of the bends of the river someone
had recently caught a Chinook salmon and it was
still alive on the bar not far from the road.

Reed bounced on the seat and pointed at everything he liked as they went. He especially liked
the salmon and wanted Talon to stop and get a
closer look.

The fisherman was a young man who had come
all the way up from Bear Valley to go fishing. The
salmon was a nice fifteen-pounder and Reed was

totally impressed. He poked a little at its eyes and raked a little with his fingernails at the scales and jumped back in surprise when it lifted its tail and flopped over.

"You should do this Talon," said Aggie, "I would like a nice fish dinner and I could can some. Mom would love some too. Dad still fishes when he can. You should have him show you how he gets them. Reed would love it."

Talon looked at the fisherman and then at the fish. It did look like fun.

"Well, guess we could," he said. "Might be kinda fun."

"Ya!" said Reed. "Fun! Get one now?"

"Not now buddy," said Talon, "got to get to town."

Reed looked at Aggie with begging eyes and silently mouthed "Please". Aggie smiled and pointed to the buckboard. Talon was saying goodbye to the fisherman.

The rest of the trip went just as planned. The

horses seemed to be content, and even Reed was slowing down. Chipmunks and ground squirrels ran across the road and made him call out in excitement, and magpies and crows called out from the trees. Every jackrabbit that they saw sent Reed's puppy to the end of his rope whining and barking to chase it. Doves cooed from the branches of the trees as they passed.

Talon had become fairly good with the 38 he bought from Joseph Long. It went where he went. He didn't like showing it off so he kept it under the seat of the wagon, but it was never far from reach. Today he even had the shotgun under the seat.

In town, the first thing on the list was the General Store. The streets were full of people as they rode past the hotel and on to the store. Lacey was serving coffee to a customer as they passed and happened to look out the window. She smiled when she saw who it was.

Talon was looking at the hotel. It had new paint, and painted on one of the windows were the words:

West Branch Hotel and Restaurant. He wasn't looking inside. "Look at that," he said, "we got a restaurant now. Maybe we should drop in while we are in
town."

Aggie was looking at it also. "I think we should,"
she said.

Talon drove the wagon down Main Street to the
store and tied off at the hitching post. A few minutes
later, he was loading sixty-pound sacks of chicken
feed into the back of the wagon. Shadow hopped up
on the feed sacks and sat proudly down like he
thought they had been put there just for him.

Reed stood on the seat of the buckboard to sur-
vey the street from a better vantage point. He
watched Talon come and go from the feed storage
room adjacent to the store. The wagon was about
half loaded and Talon was arranging the load to ride
better. He was working with his back to the boardwalk when a woman's voice came from behind him.

"I told you I would," it said.

Talon recognized her voice as soon as she spoke.

He pushed one of the bags farther into the wagon for an instant while he tried to think what he should do next. *Guess I should have known.* He told himself. "Lacey Clanton!" he said before he turned around. "I thought you might have given up after all this time."

Lacey was dressed in a full-length stone grey cotton dress with a black shawl. Her long blond hair fell over it like strands of golden silk and reflected the sun so that some of the hair looked almost like you could see through it. Her bright blue eyes were smiling that famous Lacey smile that Talon remembered as well as he remembered the sound of wind in the trees. She had slipped up on him while he worked and waited for the moment she wanted. Just like always, thought Talon.

"Giving up would be a new thing for me," she said. "I don't think I would like it much. You look good. I hear you got yourself married though. Just couldn't wait for me I see. Well, I can't wait to meet her."

Her voice sounded excited and happy. She wanted to throw her arms around him and hug him like a lost family member, but she wasn't sure of her limits yet. Talon was smiling at her. He could scarcely believe she was standing in front of him. In spite of himself, he was glad to see her.

He remembered that on the night before he left her father's little ranch, Lacey had stated her position. She sat in the dark on his bunk and said that if he wouldn't take her with him she would just follow him. He had been surprised to find her in his room that night, but not as surprised as he was to hear her voice behind him today.

She began to feel a little out of place and didn't know exactly what she should do next. She smiled at Talon for a second and then directed her attention to Reed.

Reed was watching her from his standing position on the seat.

"Friend of yours?" She asked. She was close to the wagon.

"That's Reed," said Talon, "my son."

Lacey reached her right hand up to shake Reed's.

"Hello," she said to Reed. "I'm the shadow that the sun never sets on. You can call me Miss Lacey."

Talon began to get his head back in order. Lacey had surprised him and he needed time to put it all together. It really was Lacey. She really had followed him and he began to hope that didn't mean that she still had some ideas about him and her. He liked Lacey, and he was even glad to see her, but things were different now. He had Aggie, and that's who he wanted. It was a little worrisome to hear her say she was the shadow that the sun never set on. He wondered what she had on her mind. He knew Lacey well enough to know that she was very serious about the things she said. He hoped he wouldn't have to offend her, but his family was his line in the sand. This far and no further.

Reed cautiously gave her his hand. She was wearing black silk gloves that had sparkling little amethyst stones dangling on small gold chains from the cuffs. When she tried to pull her hand back Reed held onto it and twisted it a little to make the sun reflect off the stones better.

"You like them?" She asked Reed.

He answered without looking at her. "Them's purdy," he said, in a somewhat subdued voice.

"They are pretty," came a stone cold voice from the doorway of the store. It was Aggie, and she was staring at Lacey. Reed heard his mother's voice and looked over at her. She didn't look very happy.

"They are." He said carefully.

Talon and Lacey both turned to look at Aggie. Talon felt her eyes better than he heard her voice. He felt like he had been caught at something. Aggie wasn't mad but she was guarded, to say the least.

She was wearing a red gingham dress that stopped just above her ankles and showed her black leather lace-up boots under them. Her hair was tied up and her dark eyes were as alert as a lion's, ready to pounce. She was a somewhat small woman, but she was fearless when it came to her family, especially Talon.

Lacey knew instantly that she was standing on sacred ground and didn't want to cross any lines. She looked over at Talon.

"Aggie!" said Talon. "Come meet an old friend of mine. This is Lacey Clanton. I once worked for her father in South Dakota. Lacey, this is my beautiful wife Aggie."

Aggie stepped out onto the boardwalk and walked to the wagon. She pushed up against Talon and put her arm around his. She tried to smile. She was usually an easy person to talk to and made friends easily, but on her own time and turf. This time she had spotted Talon talking to a strange, very well dressed blond with her hair down, while she wasn't looking.

Times were changing. More and more women were wearing their hair down. It was one of those things Aggie hated about more people showing up in Cougar Rock. To her, it was a questionable way for a woman to act. In the bigger cities, they were raising their skirts higher as well and cutting off their hair. She liked the old way. It was more respectful.

She withheld her judgment on Lacey for now, but mostly because Lacey seemed to know Talon, even though it did make her wonder. She was wise enough to know that men were men and women were created to be able to manipulate their way around their defenses. Fortunately, She knew Talon enough to trust him, even if she didn't trust Lacey. He truly was a rock. He was her rock, and that's how she meant to keep things.

It was Reed who broke the ice. "Mom," he said, "Miss Lacey, see." He was pointing his finger at the little stones sparkling in the sun against Lacey's black gloves.

"They are very nice," Aggie said. She brushed the gathering black flies from before her eyes and extended her hand to Lacey.

"Pleased to meet you," she said. "Talon told me about your parent's place. He loves the clothes your mother made for him. I have to say, the work is exceptional and so is the material. If I might ask, what drove you all the way up here to our little town?"

"That's a long story," said Lacey. "I would love to tell you about it over coffee. I own the new restaurant in the old West Branch Hotel. Actually, I own the hotel also. It would be my pleasure to buy coffee. Oh, and a little soda too. I assume it's okay for Reed to drink soda. Anyway, what do you say? It's just up the street a little."

Talon was as surprised to hear that Lacey had bought the hotel, as he had been that she had found him. He wondered how it all had come to pass.

"That would be nice," Aggie said. "We have a few small things to tend to first though. Would an hour be okay?"

"Absolutely," said Lacey. "That would be perfect." She shook Talon and Aggie's hands again and waved bye to Reed. Then she started down the boardwalk toward the saloon. "One hour," she called out over her shoulder.

Aggie watched her for a little and then lost her in the midday traffic on the boardwalk. "She seems nice," she said to Talon.

"As I remember her, she is," Talon said. He wanted to say more but decided to let Aggie draw her own conclusions. If Lacey was up to anything, Aggie would be the first to know.

CHAPTER 15

BAD NEWS IS BETTER THAN NO NEWS

Lacey almost strutted down the street. She was in very high spirits and smiled at everything she saw. That lasted for only a couple of blocks, right up until she saw Jeff. She was about to cross the street anyway. She was headed for the Anvil to invite Louis to coffee. She had grown fond of his company and felt he would be useful to set Aggie at ease. She wanted to get to know Aggie. Not because she had any real set plans, but because Aggie was part and parcel with Talon. Talon was a friend she meant to keep at all costs.

Jeff had not seen her yet. He was picking his teeth and standing on the boardwalk under the awning. Aggie waited for a buggy to go by, and crossed right behind it. A rough-looking square-jawed prospector on a mule stopped to let her pass in front of him. He had a little donkey for a pack on a rope behind him. He smiled as politely as he knew how, and what few yellowed and broken teeth he had came out of hiding and showed themselves like they were proud. They fit his heavily bearded face well enough that Lacey hardly took notice of them. She smiled back and hurried on across the street.

Usually being noticed was what Lacey lived for, but this time she hoped she had blended into the crowd enough to escape Jeff. In a mining town the size of Cougar Rock, that would have been difficult at best. There were lots of other women in town but few had long bright blond hair that was always clean and always down.

Her hair caught in the wind and lifted a little as she moved. The prospector sat still and stared at her the whole time she was crossing. She wished he wouldn't have. It made her that much more notice-able. She hadn't gone twenty feet down the street on the other side before Jeff was standing in the walk in front of her. If she had made it thirty more feet, she would have been inside the Anvil.

"I'm not mad," said Jeff, "in fact I kinda under-stand. I might have crossed the line a little."

I can translate that a little better, thought Lacey. What you mean to say is I need your help enough to eat a little crow to get it. "What is it, Jeff? I'm in a hurry," she said.

"Well if you want to cut right to the chase, then okay." Jeff said, "That friend of yours, Talon. He found a lot of gold in a cave in that mountain he lives on. Now that gold has no claim on it, cause I checked. I got as far as that big iron door he has. I know it was his, cause he came in with some other guy while I was there and I had to leave.

"It's a long slow trip, and a dangerous one, even with good light. I need a better way. Now, I can't seem to find that door anywhere I looked outside, so it must be inside the house somewhere.

"I also need to know where to go from there. Could be one of three ways. I know the Indian ain't going to help me, but you could. You could find out from him. Now before you get all upset, just you think about it. This thing could make us both rich. It made that Indian rich and he only got a little of it. Now I'm not goin to wait for you to start screaming and kicking about it. I'm leaving for now. You just think about it."

Jeff turned on his heel and headed back across the street. Lacey wondered what his hurry was until she turned around to go on to the Anvil, and saw Louis coming from the corner near the Anvil. He had been facing Jeff and when he saw who he was talking to, he started their way making tracks. He smiled at Lacey when he got up to her.

"You okay?" He said.

"I'm fine. You have great timing."

Louis was feeling like he had a lot better ground

to stand on these days, and he didn't like Jeff hounding Lacey. If he could have caught up in time he would have said as much to his face, but that would have to wait. He stood close to her and looked into her eyes. Jeff was becoming a problem. In one way he was glad. It made his presence more needed, but in another, it worried him. He had no idea how dangerous Jeff might be, and he had no way of finding out unless Lacey would open up and tell him. They had been seeing each other long enough to give him the right to know.

Lacey looked up into his gentle stone grey eyes and knew what he was thinking. She wasn't ready to tell him about what Jeff really wanted, that was more to do with Talon anyway, but what she knew would come out sooner or later. She might just as well tell him now.

She decided to wait and tell Talon and Aggie at the same time. Talon was more than just a casual friend, and he had proven himself to be a fearless man in her eyes. She might need all the help she could get. The last thing she wanted was to have him think she was in some way working with Jeff.

She had already thought it through the first time she met Jeff at the saloon. They had both showed up in town about the same time. That would make the lie Jeff threatened about her and Talon all that much easier for folks to believe. Things were getting a little tangled, and she was starting to feel all alone in a sort of way. Being near Louis made her feel more like she had people she could confide in. What she needed was a way to bind them all together before Jeff could tear them apart.

"Louis," she said, "I know what you're thinking and I can't keep it from you any longer. It would be unfair. We need to talk. I'm meeting Talon and Aggie Windcatcher at the hotel for coffee in a few minutes. I came to get you to be with me. I will tell you then. Can we go?" Now that she had decided she wanted to tell, she didn't want to wait any longer. She might change her mind, and that wouldn't do.

Louis was all but smitten by her request. She had come to him for his company. Jeff had obviously not been part of her plan. It made him feel like she was his. He hoped he was right.

Lacey was silent on the walk back to the hotel. She looked a little worried to Louis. He noticed her expression and decided to let her alone.

Talon and Aggie hadn't arrived yet so Lacey went to the kitchen and found some cookies she had recently made. She left Louis at the same table they used the day he found the menu. She had decided it was her favorite table and never used it for customers. There were little reminders on small pieces of paper, and pencils scattered about on the table. He pushed them to the middle of the table to make room for Talon and Aggie.

Louis knew Tom Stonewell better than he did Talon, but he did a lot of business with Talon and liked him. Tom Stonewell was Aggie's father. Louis had spent a few days in high country with him and had since become close friends with his family.

Lacey returned to the table with the cookies and decided to wait for Talon and Aggie before she brought the coffee. She seemed preoccupied. She sat down next to Louis to wait without saying anything. He could see that she was bothered but he didn't know why. She let her hair fall forward like a curtain and began doodling on one of the pieces of paper that was on the table.

It was enough to be next to her and Louis was patient to wait. After a few minutes, she sat up a little straighter and pulled her hair back. She smiled at Louis. "Sorry," she said, "didn't mean to ignore you."

Louis just smiled at her. She sat back in her chair and reached over to Louis's lap and took his hand in hers. She put it in her lap and held it with both of her hands.

She had decided to tell something that she had hoped would never come up and no one would ever need to know. Recent events had changed things. If she tried to keep it secret any longer it might mean

Jeff would have it to use to manipulate her. It wasn't something she liked knowing herself, much less telling someone else. She was only worried about her closest friends. She didn't have enough of them to waste any.

If Jeff got to them first it might look like she was hiding other things as well, things that never happened but could be made to look more believable. She was mostly worried about Talon. Jeff's threat of spreading rumors about them was not just a threat. She thought about it and realized that he might be desperate enough over the gold to try anything.

Aggie, she didn't know at all, but she was Talon's wife and that was enough. Lacey already had plans of getting close to her, so she could stay friends with Talon without making it look bad. Louis was the other friend she was worried about hurting. Jeff would get to him too if he could.

She was falling in love with Louis. He was like a big soft teddy bear that had real teeth. His laugh was contagious for her and she loved his eyes. They were gentle-looking most of the time. When they weren't, they turned cold as steel, like you might see on an animal. She had seen those eyes the day she slapped Jeff at the saloon. Thinking about him made her smile over at him. He squeezed her hand and smiled back.

Talon and Aggie walked in off the boardwalk and a few black flies came in with them. The day was hot and the tiny black flies were anywhere there were horses.

The old saloon dog had been drawn by the smell of food and changed his preferred place of interest. He tried to enter the restaurant with Talon and Aggie. Aggie cut him off with her knee and made him stay outside. Reed wanted to pet him but he was ushered into the shade of the restaurant by Aggie. He looked out the big window to the buckboard to check up on Shadow. He spotted him sitting on the seat watching them from outside.

"You made it," said Lacey cheerfully. "I assume you both know Louis already."

"Sure we do," Said Talon.

They sat down across the table from Lacey and Louis. Lacey offered them some of the cookies, which Reed thought of as right neighborly, and happily sat down next to Aggie to eat one. Lacey left to get the coffee.

"Good seeing you Louis," said Talon. He was a little relieved to see that Lacey had a male friend. It made him smile at Aggie. She caught the silent statement and smiled back.

Louis seemed a little embarrassed but happy.

"So, how is the restaurant's food?" Talon asked.

"Best in town," said Louis. "A lot better than I ever had before. Course, it wouldn't take a lot to beat the saloon."

Lacey returned with the coffee. She had left it on the back of the stove so it was already hot. She poured a round for everyone and gave Reed the root beer she brought with her. She got the nod of approval from Aggie. Reed was beginning to think this Lacey person was almost as important as Shadow. He even liked her restaurant.

Lacey sat down next to Louis and took his hand in both of hers again. She held it in her lap. Lacey wasn't sure how to begin. She felt like she was moving a little too fast, but she knew Jeff a lot better than she wished she did. It really wasn't anyone's business but hers, but she worried that it would be sooner then she wanted. It wasn't a big deal anyway. They wouldn't even care unless Jeff used it to hurt her.

The gold in Talon's cave was another matter she planned to talk about. Talon needed to know, especially if Jeff started sniffing around their house. She had started the day thinking she was only needing to talk about her and Jeff. Now she was glad she had run into Jeff. That would be another thing she would need to share.

Small talk started and rambled from the dead insurance man, to the hotel, and then to the salmon. Lacey let the time slip past and they drank coffee and had a few laughs for a while.

It was good to see Talon, and Lacey had already started liking Aggie. She felt an odd sort of kinship to her, like they were somehow bonded through Talon. Aggie laughed easily and had intelligence she related to. They seemed to think a lot alike.

It was Louis who started the more serious talk. He remembered that she had promised to tell him about Jeff. He looked over at her and squeezed her hand a little to get her attention.

Jeff was becoming a problem, and Louis needed to know how big a problem. She looked over at him and saw that he was tired of waiting. At least that's how it seemed. She looked back at the rest of the table. Everyone was looking at her like they had run out of something to say. Lacey braced herself and then began.

"I have something I would like to share," she said. "There has been a man in town you may have seen, a tall, blond man with blue eyes. Likes to sneak around, and wears black clothes a lot."

Aggie knew who she meant. The image of him standing and waving at her from the bridge instantly came to mind. It brought her to full attention.

Lacey continued. "He is here trying to get anything he can, and he don't mind breaking all the rules he needs to in order to get it. Right now, he is after the gold in your cave, Talon. The reason I know this is because he has approached me for how he might be able to do that. The reason he approached me, is because I'm your friend. He was one of my mother's lovers years ago. I don't know how he got to Cougar Rock and I don't care. He thinks I can help him get information about the gold that is in the cave. There is another reason he came to me. A reason I wish I could change. His name is Jeffery Baker, and 'he' is where I got my blond hair and blue eyes."

She stopped talking for a moment to let that soak in and then went on. "I wouldn't want you to think he was ever a father to me, quite the opposite actually. What he was, and for all I know still is, is one of my loving mother's other lovers. He is the only one I ever met and I didn't even know about him being my biological father until after my real father sold the ranch. By real, I mean the man who raised me.

"The man who raised me was Ed Clanton. I have his last name because he earned the right to give it to me. He is the only father I have. I always just thought that Jeff was one of Mom's lovers. She told me otherwise on the day I left Wolf Creek.

"The reason I wanted to tell you about him, is because he might try to use his position to convince you that we are together on his evil little plan. "Right now you are the only people in my life that I call my friends, and anything that would harm our friendship is of foremost importance to me. So there you have it. If he shows up, he is not part of me in any way. If I had my way, Jeff Baker would not exist. But, there are only so many things one can control. Jeff is not one of them."

The table was silent for a while. Business had been good and Lacey had hired Seth Jackson to wait tables and help around the hotel. He looked over at the table and Lacey waved him away.

He was clearing the dishes off another table and Lacey watched him secret out a piece of ham that had been left. On the way to the kitchen, he slipped out the new swinging doors that led to the back of the hotel past the old cell. The old dog suddenly left off watching through the front window and trotted around the hotel to the back door where Seth put the ham for him. A moment later Seth came back through the doors again and held them so that they would not make noise as they closed. He wasn't sure Lacey would like him feeding the old dog, because he had become a bit of a nuisance, always trying to sneak in through the door out front.

He had befriended the dog because he had been hungry and rejected himself in times past and felt sorry for him. They had become good friends.

Part of Seth's pay was meals for him and his father Dexter. A large shadow blocked the door as Dexter came in for that very purpose. He took off his hat and hung it on the rack by the door. He was looking around for a table he liked and saw the table where Lacey and Louis were sitting. He recognized Talon and Aggie and smiled over at them. Lacey knew she was about to be needed in the kitchen. She was hoping for some feedback before she left.

Aggie was the first to say anything. "I have seen him around our house and now I know why," Aggie said.

Talon was starting to steam. This was good information, but it was bad news. He knew someone had been snooping around and now he had a name. He wasn't sure of the law about the gold under the cabin. There was a chance that it was not technically on his land. It was under it, and that should make it his without a claim. He decided that he should go by the courthouse and find out anyway.

The gold he had found while they were lost, he reasoned was his as well. He found it. It should be like any other claim. The fact that he wasn't working it was of no consequence. He found it. He couldn't claim it legally, for not knowing where it was on the map. For that same reason, nobody else could claim it either. Besides that, the chances of anyone finding it were small at best.

He remembered what Aggie and he had gone through to get there themselves.

Even if they did find it, they would never live to spend it. If he and Aggie had not been tied together and he had not been anchored they would have both washed over the falls and into the belly of the earth someplace. Every detail of their escape had been perfect. Even the bear. That was a thing he had pondered many times, that bear. In any case, he knew nobody finding that gold would ever spend it.

Worse than the gold was how he felt about the rest of the cave. It was more like a gravesite than a cave to him. Some of his own people were buried there. To think of someone wandering around down there disturbed him, especially since he knew there was no way to stop them.

Jeff had been in there and he would not be the last. He found it unnerving to think that a strange man was watching his house and creeping around under it. He wasn't sure what he could do about that, but he was sure he would do something. He looked over at Reed who smiled back at him. He wasn't sure what something would be, but if something left another body laying around Cougar Rock, it would be a body no one would ever find.

Talon and Aggie left the restaurant in the heat of the afternoon. The street was a small storm of dust that blew along the boardwalk. Nothing else but the people and horses moved. It was the heat of the day and nature shut down till evening. Even the crows had found hiding places out of the direct sun.

His team stood with their heads down and dozed while they waited. Shadow had taken refuge under the seat. The sun heated the ground to the point that the dust in the street was hot to the touch.

Louis stepped out and stopped to adjust to the heat for a moment. He waved at Talon and started down the street. A few miners left the General Store as one of Dan's freight wagons arrived to offload supplies from Bear Valley. They kicked up more dust as they moved through the street. Talon loaded Aggie and Reed into the wagon and set out for home.

The ride home was silent. Talon was thinking of all that the day had brought. He was still a little shocked to have seen Lacey in town, much less the owner of the hotel. She had already made it modern looking. From the inside, it didn't even resemble the old hotel. And if that wasn't shocking enough, the rodent that had been watching him and his family was her father. Cougar Rock was becoming a little too crowded for him.

He liked Lacey and was glad there was a decent place to eat now. He had to admit that he was glad to see her again. He was especially glad that Louis had seen her first. Them being together was a good thing. She hadn't made it a crowded place any more than all the rest. It was just all of them together, and now Jeffery.

As the wagon passed the round pen, Talon

looked over at the barn. He was looking for anything out of place but found nothing. It felt good to be home, but the quiet, safe feeling was gone. Now he suspected everything. He hated looking over his shoulder all the time, but that's how it looked like things were going to be for awhile.

Chapter 16

Riders in the Night

The day was coming to a close, and Jeff was getting anxious about the gold in the cave. He had marked his way from the grave to the iron door with white chalk. It was several miles of great places to die. He literally had to climb up a small waterfall in one place not far from the entry.

Other places had intersecting shafts that he walked past going in, and then he wasn't sure if they were the right way out coming back. At one point, if he had not found a dead flashlight battery he had discarded, he would have turned the opposite direction of where he needed to go.

Finding the right way meant trying different shafts for a short way without marking them, and then returning before he could get confused to where he had last marked the wall and working from there. The work had been slow and threatening. It took the best part of a day to find his way back.

He needed two things. One was access to that door. The other was some way to know what direction Talon had taken after that. He could go on any one of the choices from the door, but the chances of getting lost were high. Even with good light, he might find other places like some of the ones he had already seen, where the shaft was a dead end or a drop into a hole. In one of the shafts he explored, he came to a wall that looked like a dead end and then discovered that the shaft went straight up for about thirty feet. The walls were too smooth to climb and it cost him a half-day of work to get back to where the marked shaft started.

He had discovered another problem with the cave as well. Even being as careful as he could, he would now and then come onto a shaft that entered the one he was in at a steep angle and it had slipped past him going in. If he had not chalked the wall close to where the shaft happened by accident, he had no way of knowing which way he needed to go. He had worked his way down the new shaft a little way and couldn't find any chalk mark. That let him think he was going the wrong way so he tried to backtrack himself, only to find another shaft had slipped by on his way up the new one.

That was the day he had found the dead battery. The last shaft he had wandered into happened to cross the original one. It saved his life.

He had developed a strong respect for the mountain's ability to confuse him, and it would only take one slip to end his life. At some point, he would run out of batteries, and if he didn't fall to his death in one of the drop holes, he might just as well shoot himself.

So far, all he had was the word of one of the miners who knew the story of Talon's gold from someone else, but the proof was in Talon himself. Talon had nothing the last time Jeff saw him. Now he had land and a new house. Not to mention, a very nice start for a horse ranch.

Jeff rode down the river road in the fading light on his way to Talon's barn. It was the only place left where the iron door could be. If it turned out not to be there, then it would mean that he had been right about it being in the house someplace.

The sun had set by the time he got to within sight of the barn. The last of the light was dying and he needed to wait for full dark. The last thing he wanted was to get caught snooping around on Talon's land. He had his flashlight and had discovered that a red handkerchief held over the lens gave enough light to see by, but was harder to see from a distance. The red light didn't carry well and would make him less noticeable.

He hoped Talon would be home by this time of

the day having supper. Any other day he would have been, but the trip home today had made him late, and he was still feeding when Jeff pulled up to wait.

Talon saw him coming before he stopped to wait. He watched him ride up the road far enough to identify his wing-footed horse. Now that he was closer he could see that it also was built downhill and had a Roman nose. There was only one person it could be. He tried to study the face but the light was too poor. He was in the loft when he saw Jeff. He had been throwing hay out for a mare he was working with. Now he watched from a crack in one of the wallboards.

As he watched, the light in the sky died out. The evening doves had come in to roost and the chickens hopped up onto the stall rails and settled in for the night.

Talon stood still and waited. He could see the bridge even in the poor light. Light from the house reflected off it enough to keep watch that Jeff couldn't cross it unseen. It wasn't a long wait. He heard Jeff's horse plod up to the round pen and stop. A minute later he saw a red light moving around the curve of the pen. He was surprised to see the red light. He didn't know what to expect, but maybe a small white light. He couldn't remember ever seeing a red light before. The night had gotten dark a little early due to a temporary overcast. The moon hadn't risen yet, and it gave Jeff a little advantage. Talon still had the advantage of surprise.

Quiet steps moved into the large door of the barn under where Talon was standing. Jeff was shining the light all around looking for anything that might be a way to hide the door. Talon waited until he walked past under him and then fired the 38 into the ground just behind the light.

Pine chips used for bedding on the floor scattered in all directions, some of them hitting Jeff's legs and lower body with enough force to sting. The chickens blew up in a panic and one of them flew blindly into the back of his head and bounced off. All the doves in the loft flew into the darkness at once.

Jeff dove for cover. He wasn't sure if he had been shot or not. The chicken he figured out soon enough but he had dropped his light and dove for cover up against one of the stall gates. It wasn't much but in a panic, it was all he had. He threw up his arm to deflect any other attackers and gathered his senses for an instant. The light had fallen to the ground ten feet behind him. He needed it back and started to crawl over to it.

"Leave it," came Talon's voice. "Won't do you any good in hell anyway."

The light was shining in Jeff's face. He put his right hand up to block it, but not before Talon saw his face. He had seen Jeff's face before, but it had been a long time back. He tried to place where.

"You ain't going to make very many friends like that," said Jeff."

"When I need new friends I'll buy more horses," said Talon.

"Well," said Jeff, "I hope you wouldn't shoot a man just for looking for a place to sleep for the night."

"Ya," said Talon. "Is that what you were doing on the hill beside my house and in the shaft under it? Looking for a place to sleep?"

Jeff was caught, but he wasn't ready to admit to anything. "You sure you got the right man?" he said.

"I'm sure," said Talon. "I'm sure of something else too. I'm sure that if I find you under my house or watching it again I won't be shooting to warn you."

Jeff wasn't worried about being shot. At least not where he sat. He felt for the lump inside the top of his boot and wondered if he would need what was kept there. He decided that he was safe enough for the moment. He wasn't so sure about what might happen if he was caught under Talon's house, but that was to be thought out later.

He wished he could somehow break the ice with Talon. It seemed impossible but at the moment he decided he might as well try. "Well, I thought you might be a little more sociable to an old acquaintance. Last time we met, you and your friend got off with my rifle. That should buy a guy a 'little' tolerance shouldn't it?"

Talon was silent. Jeff stood carefully up and wiped some of the dust off his pants.

"You're after my gold," Talon said. He remembered the rifle and now he had a face for the name.

"Well, I'm after 'some' gold. You can't claim the whole mountain," Jeff said. "I don't care about the little stream you been working; that ain't what I'm after. But you can't control the entire mountain just because you found gold in part of it. Anyway, Why fight over it? It's a big mountain."

Talon knew Jeff was right. He really had no law that let him control the whole mountain. He couldn't even stop people from finding his shaft under the house. What he could control was the entry to it. That was his alone. He had visited the courthouse on his way home and even though it seemed a little silly, he had placed an official claim on the gold under the house. It gave him several acres of land in all directions from his house.

"Maybe I can't control the whole mountain," said Talon. "What I can do, is shoot anyone I find down there on my claim, and getting rid of a body would be an easy thing in a place like that. Who could say what happened to them? Must have just gotten lost."

Jeff knew he was right about that. He wondered if Talon had what it would take to actually kill someone, but that didn't matter at the moment either. "I ain't aimin' to hurt your family. Fact is, I couldn't care less about them. But what harm would it do for you to let me just use your iron door to come and go from? Wouldn't that just be more neighborly of ya?"

Talon had no intention of letting Jeff or anyone else into his cave if he could stop them. Even if Jeff had come to him first he wouldn't have let him in. He would have a much higher opinion of him though. As it stood, he saw Jeff as a sneak and a thief.

Jeff started looking for his hat and found it over by the light. He knew that Talon wasn't going to shoot him so he walked over and picked it up. He picked up the light at the same time.

"You ain't usin' my door," said Talon, "and you better not get caught under my house again either. You can find some other way. All the gold I found is mine by rights. So even if you could find it you would be a claim jumper. As far as the rest of the mountain goes, it's your hide. If you think you can find your way in and out of it, go right ahead. Just do it someplace else. I will kill you for snooping around my family."

Jeff could tell that Talon was not bluffing about his family. He might not kill over the cave, but the sound of his voice when he mentioned his family had a different ring to it.

"Well no hard feelins," said Jeff. "I can see you ain't in no mood to be polite tonight, so if it's all good to you I think I might just as well be on my way."

"You do that," said Talon, "if you do happen to get rich, maybe you should come by and buy a horse. That thing your riding is breaking down your image."

Jeff couldn't tell, but Talon was smiling. He didn't say anything about the horse. It wasn't important. Besides he knew Talon was right. But he had what he could get, and it still beat walking. He slapped the dust off his hat and walked out of the barn.

Talon listened for his footfalls until he got back to his horse and rode away. He thought about the posse, and remembered Jeff's face. He wasn't very happy-looking then either. It amazed him how gold attracted people.

He expected strangers, but lately, it seemed like everyone he met came out of his past. He thought of Domingo and was glad he had landed in Cougar Rock. He would know Jeff, and Talon made a mental note to go see the sheriff. He wanted to know how dangerous he thought Jeff might be. Lacey sure had nothing good to say about him. He also wondered why a sneak and a thief wasn't carrying a gun. It dawned on him that just because he didn't see one, didn't mean there wasn't one.

CHAPTER 17

THE EYE IN THE SKY

Axle Ford rode up the narrow road that led to Cougar Rock. He had been in Bear Valley, snooping. It had rained most of the night and the road was still wet. Puddles ran long in the tracks of the wagons that worked up and down it every day. He noticed a couple of swans eating mosquitoes in a small meadow lake that was not more than a bog most of the year. It was holding a lot of water now. Ducks swam near them and pushed their heads under the water for the new sprouts that the warm weather had started on the bottom of the pond. Mosquitoes buzzed around

his head and kept him swatting at them as they landed on his face. They were almost a blanket on his
horse's face and made him keep shaking his head.
The ones on the horse's eyes were red with blood
and more were waiting for those to drop off.

It was early; Axle wished for the sun to get hot
and burn off the bugs. It wouldn't have any effect
on the ever-present black flies and horse flies, but
the mosquitoes would give up and hide out if it got
hot enough.

He looked at the sky and wondered if he would
see the sun at all. Dark clouds hung overhead and
bulged out at the bottoms like they were over-full
with water. They looked low and blocked out the
rising sun that should have been bright half an
hour ago. The bugs, on days like this one, were almost unbearable.

Dragonflies buzzed by in uncountable numbers
eating the mosquitoes and gnats. He liked the colors
of the large blue and red dragonflies. They were an
amazing insect that could outfly most of all the other

insects he knew. Damselflies were also common near the water but much smaller.

The sound of blackbirds came from all directions. They were red wing or yellow and were always singing. One he noticed had caught a dragonfly and sat on the top of a cattail bulb showing it off like a trophy before he ate it. They were congregated in the dead willow trees that stood along the edge of the little puddle. The road would soon lead past the little swamp and the bugs would lessen, but after a night rain they would still be a big problem for a while.

Where he was headed, it wouldn't be as bad though. It made it easier to put up with. The day gained light, but the clouds only lifted a little. They still looked close enough to shoot a hole through. He rode through the mud and water for another hour and came to the Clearwater River. It was swollen from the rain, but not badly.

He was below the crossing but had crossed where he was before. His horse was strong and could swim well. Axle put his knees up onto the top of the saddle and let his feet hang over the rump of the horse to keep them dry as he crossed. The water where he crossed was swift and deep but the river was split by an island in the middle. Crossing at the downstream end of the island, the bar was wider and more shallow.

He crossed over and headed straight up the mountain on the other side. It was a steep climb and the horse could only make it up part way to where he wanted to go. He left it hobbled where he always left it and continued on foot.

There was an almost constant breeze where the horse was. It was steep and high but worth the hour or so ride up. He had found a little knoll with grass to leave his horse and the wind kept the mosquitoes blown away. There weren't as many to start with that high up the hill.

The horse was lathered with sweat from the climb. Axle was glad to be able to get the saddle off him and let him cool down. After he hobbled the horse he took the saddlebags off the saddle and set out. He climbed a little higher to get over a rock out-cropping, and then dropped down to a lower spot where a large blue spruce lived. It was good cover and he lit a little fire under the canopy of its bows and started a small pot of coffee.

From where he sat, he could see the entire town of Cougar Rock and a good bit of the river beyond. He could also see where he crossed the river but that wasn't of any importance at the moment. He pulled a nice looking monocular from his saddlebag and watched the little town start up while he waited for his coffee.

The spot he wanted to see was in the crossing. It was Douglas Brogan's abandoned camp and he could see it well. From looking down on it, all that was hidden was a small section of river right below him. He scoped the camp and the crossing for a while and spotted a prospector still trying the gravel in the bars along the islands.

He had been to the Bear Valley Hardware look-ing for anything he might find out about Jeff. He found nothing there. That was where most of the town's guns were sold, and he hoped he would learn something from them. From there, he went to the post office. If Jeff was receiving any mail, he wasn't getting it in Cougar Rock. He had to show his badge, but he discovered that someone fitting Jeff's description had picked up a package there a week or so before.

The name on the box it was sent to was Douglas Brogan. The man who picked up the order had the key to Brogan's box and got the slip there to get the package. It was too large for the post office box so they left a pickup slip in the box for the key bearer to find.

The clerk remembered giving the man the box because he wasn't someone he had seen before. Bear Valley was a pretty large town and most of the people simply came and went unnoticed. This one seemed nervous. He hurried in and left as soon as he got the package.

The clerk had not noticed where the box had been sent from when he handed it over, and the man who received it wasn't talking about it. In fact, he was almost rude in his hurry to get out of the post office.

That was an interesting bit of information. Someone was using the dead man's post office box. *Must not want to use their own name,* thought Axle. But that didn't make a lot of sense either. Why would they want to use Brogan's? The thought came to him that if it was Jeff he might want to keep his business out of Cougar Rock for unknown reasons. If he was broke and couldn't rent a box, but had the key available, he would use it if he needed something bad enough.

That made the only sense he could think of. In any case, he now believed more than ever that Jeff was involved in the killing of Brogan. At the stable, he learned that a man could have sold a horse there and it would mean nothing. They sold and bought horses every day. The bill of sale would have been handed off to the new owner as soon as one could be found.

Axle wished he could have gotten more information than that. He suspected that Jeff had sold Brogan's horse soon after the shooting. The horse had never showed up in the area. He also thought of visiting the Nez Perce reservation to look for the horse over there, but it had been a while since it would have been sold, and would be hard to find even if it had gone to the Indians. Besides that, he had no way of knowing what the animal looked like. All he could do is ask if a new horse had shown up about the time of the shooting. He figured they would be mum about it if they did know.

Overall, it had been a profitable trip. Now he wanted more, and from where he was he could get it.

The breeze blew the limbs of the spruce and moved the buffalo grass on the hill he was on and blew against the little fire under the tree. He poured a cup of coffee and went back to watching. A flock of mallard ducks flew by just under him. They were flying low to stay under the ceiling that the clouds created. Their wings whistled in the damp, cool morning air. He watched them pass and marveled at the colors of the males. They were only about fifty feet below him, not more than a hundred feet off the tops of the trees on the river. The clouds were lifting a little and moving off and his coffee tasted heavenly. It all held the promise of a good day.

Axle rested against the steep slope of the hill and waited. Now and then he saw something he was interested in and spotted it with the monocular. He had finished his coffee and was feeling a little chill in the breeze. He thought of giving up and going in for something to eat at the West Branch when something moved directly below him.

Another small flock of ducks flew by and whistled with the rhythm of their wings as they went. He was looking at them when suddenly he spotted a man on the bank of the river. The man was walking up the riverbank on his side of the river. He came from the bottom of the hill on foot and must have been camped there.

The man disappeared into a willow thicket where large willow trees had created a thick canopy. He came out with a horse. Axle was amazed he had not seen it. Then he realized that he hadn't been looking anyplace downriver from the crossing. The man led the horse back to where he came from and disappeared again under the hill Axle was on. He watched the spot for a little while and saw the man ride out on the horse. He had saddled it at a camp Axle could not see from where he was. It was too close to the bottom of the hill and the hill hid the spot.

The man rode the horse upriver and into the water. He crossed to the first island and moved upstream as he crossed to the next. From there he went straight to Brogan's camp.

CHAPTER 18

DEAD DRUNK

Jeff Baker heard the same flock of ducks. He looked up at them and thought of how he might kill one without shooting and drawing a lot of attention to himself.

He was broke again and decided that if Douglas' saddle was still there he would ride it down to Bear Valley and sell it. He left his horse tied to a willow tree and went on into the camp on foot. The saddle was gone. He figured someone else could have grabbed it but then remembered the empty casing for the .35 the sheriff had. No doubt he was the one who took the saddle.

Jeff would have sold the saddle with the horse but he worried about blood. He looked for any he could find but there wasn't any. It still unnerved him and the buyer didn't need a saddle anyway.

The whole mess unnerved him. He looked around the camp and began to remember Doug Brogan. He missed him. They had been partners for almost two years and he had gotten to know him. He was a smart man and a good talker.

They hit Cougar Rock the same way they had hit all the towns south of there. Drifted in, started a fire in someone's business, and then talked it up all around. They offered the burn victim insurance after the damage was done. He was always the last one they offered it to. That usually meant the victim would bemoan his plight to everyone they knew. Once the word got around they could sell all the phony insurance they wanted. He always wondered why people were so gullible. But he was glad they were.

On the night that Douglas died, they had been drinking. Douglas wanted to hit up Larry Adams for a sale. The fire was a few days old and he wanted the money. He was talking about getting out, and Larry was the last sucker he had on his list.

Jeff was afraid it was too soon. There were still people who they could sell to. He also thought that Adams might put two and two together if they showed up so soon after the fire. Even in a town where there was no sheriff, they had rope. Besides that, he had heard about the gold in Talon's cave. He had spotted Talon working in the round pen and knew who he was. He also knew that he was a little less than broke the last time he saw him.

He asked around and discovered that Talon had bought the land, built the bridge and the new house and then stocked the place with prize horses from the Nez Perce.

Word was that they had left the cave under the waterfall behind the Stonewell cabin, but it was impossible to go back into the cave from there due to the great river that was in the cave. It was a place where the river made a waterfall that was impossible to climb. The story had to be true and he wanted to stay and find the gold.

Douglas, when he drank, got mean, and normally Jeff left him alone and slept somewhere out of easy reach. But this time they had come back to camp together and were drinking as they rode. They tied their horses and took their saddles into the camp where Douglas built a small fire and sat watching it for a little while.

Jeff was rolling out his bed when Douglas started in. "You got no brain," he said. "You never could see past your nose. We can hit the hotel and head for someplace farther north. Even if they suspicion something we'll be gone."

He was starting to get a sneer in his voice. It was a voice Jeff had heard before. He wanted to tell Doug that the only thing that kept them ahead of the game so far was the fact that nobody had tried to claim the insurance while they were around. Taking a chance of letting the cat out of the bag while they were still in town would put the law on their heels in a few hours. The last thing he wanted was any suspicion from trying to sell insurance for the hotel so soon after the fire.

Douglas argued that they had already sold it to the rest of the town since the fire, and it wouldn't matter.

The voice Jeff was listening to was telling him that there was nothing he could say that wouldn't serve as a reason for more arguing. The arguing would only last a few minutes and then Doug would want to fight.

Jeff had let that happen once before. For a man with no brain, he had learned that lesson the first time. Douglas could fly off the ground from a dead standstill with the speed of a small bird, and the force of a runaway freight wagon. It took Jeff several weeks to heal up from the first time he tangled with Douglas, and he seemed madder now then he was then.

Douglas knew some sort of kick fighting he used, and he never used his hands. The first kick was usually all he needed. He could kick forward by leaping into the air and flying at his victim with his leg cocked like a spring on a bear trap. He could also spin and back kick but he preferred the former.

Jeff said nothing back as Douglas began his rant. What he did do was reach into his boot top and get the little pistol. It held seven rounds and he didn't plan to need even one. The threat should be enough.

Douglas was ranting on, and soon his voice began to rise to a yell. He was glaring at Jeff who was standing at the edge of camp holding the pistol in his pocket with the hammer pulled back. He carried the little gun with a round in the chamber all the time. He reasoned that if he needed it he would need it quick.

Jeff saw Douglas stand up and then he suddenly crouched a little to gather the coiled springs in his legs he had for muscle. When he did, Jeff knew what was next. He had seen it in a hundred bars farther south. He pulled the pistol from his pocket and pointed it at Douglas. He was thinking of making his case, but Douglas was already in the air. It happened so fast, that he hardly knew what did happen.

Douglas was flying at him at chest height. He was raising the pistol, though he had no intention of using it. He remembered his chest exploding with pain and flying through the air and onto the rocks of the bar, but after that, he only remembered trying to get his breath back. Douglas was drunk enough that he had hit lower than he intended and the kick caught Jeff in the chest. He was holding the pistol and when he got hit his hand closed into a fist. His finger was on the trigger when it happened.

After he was able to get his strength back he got up onto his knees and found the pistol. Then he found Douglas. He was dead. The bullet had passed through his heart as sure as if Jeff had aimed it at him.

At first, he was in a state of shock. He staggered back until he backed into a willow tree and the limbs kept him from falling. Then he dropped to his knees and tried to think what he should do next. He double-checked Douglas for life. He was not breathing and blood was running off his chest in a little rivulet that pooled in his clothes. It flowed over the small stones and sand at his side and then drained into the sand like flowing through a screen.

Jeff panicked. He had just killed Douglas. Even if he could claim self-defense it would blow the lid off their entire operation. If he didn't hang for shooting an unarmed man, he would be in prison for the rest of his life over the two things combined.

He began to sweat, it ran down from his cheekbones and started soaking his shirt at the armpits. He was in more trouble now than he had ever been in his life. He should have seen something like this coming, he told himself. But, that was no use now. He needed a way to make this all go away.

He sat for a long time trying to quiet his panic. His heart was pounding in his ears and he thought he might pass out. Blood had rushed to his head and he started feeling dizzy. He needed to gain control.

He listened to see if anyone was coming to the sound of the shot. The thought of that drove his panic harder. He jumped up and walked down the edge of the little island for a ways to see if anyone was there. As far as he could see, no one was around. The campfires of the other camps that he knew of had burned out and the miners were asleep. He stood and waited for his heart to stop pounding. It was a little easier where he didn't have to look at Douglas.

He needed a plan, and he needed it before daybreak. As well as he could guess, that would be in about three hours. He returned to the camp and looked down at Douglas one more time. Then he got busy. He kicked Douglas's saddle off the top of his and left it lying on its side. Then he took his saddle and put it on his horse and brought both horses over as close to camp as the underbrush would let him. After that, he pushed Douglas up onto the back of his horse and centered his weight.

He thought of using the saddle but he knew from experience that blood is nearly impossible to clean off leather, especially if the leather is dry and a little unkept. The stain stays for weeks, sometimes for years. He knew how to tie on a pack to the bare back of a horse and he squaw-hitched Douglas to the back of the horse.

Then he mounted his own horse and rode down the edge of the island as far out into the river as the current would let him, with Doug's horse in tow. He did the same at all the crossings in the river until he reached the other side. By that time the bleeding had slowed to only a drip or so. Once on the other side, he worked his way down the river bank out in the water until he came to the bar where the body would be found the next morning.

He returned to their camp long enough to try to hide any evidence. The bloody rocks he rolled over and the sand he scooped up and threw into the river. If the rocks were small enough they went with the sand. He threw the phony insurance contracts into the fire in a pile and looked around for anything else. He took the money from the insurance sales that Douglas had in his saddle bags. There wasn't a lot of it left.

That was when he remembered the casing. By

then he wasn't sure where he had been standing when the gun went off. He searched the ground in what little moonlight there was, and when he didn't find it he figured it must have landed in the river.

Fear and remorse soaked him to his very bones. He needed to be away, far away. He took Douglas's horse to the river and washed off all the blood he could find on him and then rode the two horses downriver a couple miles and camped up in the trees a few hundred feet from the river. He needed space and time to worry through the night's events. He needed to try to remember if anyone had seen him with Douglas in town or on the river. He searched his mind for the rest of the night, and finally fell asleep as the sun was rising.

The morning was wet and cool but the sun was gradually changing all that. Jeff had gone back to find something he could take to Bear Valley and sell. Now as he looked around the empty camp, a feeling of sadness came over him. Douglas had been a dangerous man, but he was the only friend that Jeff ever had. They understood each other. Now he was broke and alone. He thought about riding out and thought maybe he should, but to leave after all that had happened was too much. He knew the gold was there, and he knew that even Douglas would want him to stay and try to get it. *So what if it gets me killed, h*e told himself. *What else is worth dying for now?*

There was nothing left in the camp, and Jeff left again for the cemetery. He had the thought that there might be a little gold in the waterfall he had to climb to get to Talon's place. It was a long shot, but he needed to make it look like he had some reason to keep using Seth's grave hole for entry anyway. He had become so guarded about his personal business that he was skeptical of everything. He needed to look like any other miner in his mind.

He was worried that if anyone knew about the shaft going to the part of the mountain that held the gold he would be run over by starving miners. Someone else might even find it first. As long as he was working a little gravel in the shaft and bringing his tools with him as he came and went nobody would be the wiser.

He didn't know where else to go. He felt safe in the cave, and after visiting the camp again he needed to feel safe.

Axle watched Jeff ride through town. The streets had become busy but he kept his eye on Jeff with the little scope so as not to lose him. Jeff stopped his horse in front of the hotel but stayed in the middle of the street on its back. He sat for a second looking in through the window and then rode on again. When he got to the cemetery he rode through it. He rode on as far as he needed to, to hide his horse in the pines on the other side. Axle watched him disappear and come back on foot. He was only a speck even in the monocular but Axle knew it was Jeff. He never let him out of his sight.

Jeff walked past the headstones. He looked like he was carrying something in his hands but Axle could not tell what it was. He assumed it must be some kind of a ladder. The little speck of a man disappeared again when he went down the hole.

Axle knew that Jeff was the man he was looking for, but he also knew he didn't have enough proof to arrest him. So far all he had was circumstantial evidence. Even if he could connect Jeff to Douglas through the post office it would only prove that they had been friends. It wouldn't prove that Jeff killed him.

Axle smiled. Guys like Jeff were the reason he had never married or settled down. He loved his job more than he loved anything. He had spent his entire adult life tracking men like Jeff, and he caught them all. This one would be no exception. He was at the top of his game, and Jeff just made his day. He gathered his things and walked back down to his horse. He needed to report to Domingo.

CHAPTER 19

ALL THINGS COME TO ONE WHO WAITS

Lacey waited on the boardwalk. The heat of the day had mostly passed and she was waiting for Louis to bring her bay up from the stable. They planned to go riding on the other side of the river. They had become very close over the last couple months, and she was always glad to see him coming.

She had made a deal with Seth for the use of the hot water he had discovered under the hotel. She might could have claimed it without a deal, as it was under her property, but the thought never occurred to her.

The deal was simple enough. She would finance four little bathhouses with small wood stoves and cold water from the river in trade for the hot water Seth had. In the deal, the hotel would get all the hot water it needed, and Seth would pay her half his profit until the cost of the bathhouses was paid off.

The bathhouses would afford all the hot water anyone could use in a large tub for fifty cents. No time limit on how long one might stay in the water, but no overnight campers in the houses. The deal made money for the hotel and Seth. The rooms were almost never empty. Word got out and people were even coming up from Bear Valley to use the bathhouses and eat at the West Branch, or stay in one of the rooms.

Dexter had given up on prospecting. He wasn't finding enough gold to stay alive and Seth's little bathhouses were keeping them in fine shape. He started hanging out at the Anvil because the work interested him. That had worked into a job. Louis trained him to do the heavy lifting. Part of Dexter's pay was his education in the field of horse hoof trimming and shoe sizing. He also learned how to use the hearth for other iron works, and was always on hand to unload the freight wagon when fresh iron and horseshoes came in from the valley. He was filling in for Louis, who now had time to take Lacey for a ride or go for lunch, the latter he also brought back to the Anvil for Dexter.

Louis looked over at the shop as he rode out from the stable with both horses. Dexter was busy, just like he should be. Lacey smiled when he got close enough to separate him from the other movement on the street. Sometimes she could see him coming all the way from the stable. Today he was about a block away before she noticed him.

Louis dismounted when he got to the hotel and helped Lacey up on her horse. She didn't need the help but she liked the attention it afforded her. Louis liked it too. Louis tied the lunch basket on the back of his horse and they left out for a quiet dinner on the river. Dexter waved as they passed back by the Anvil on their way to the crossing.

The crossing was running clear and clean looking. The miners upriver were not affecting it like in the old days. On the other side of the river, they set out on the old trail that led to the only two cabins on that side. They intended to stop by at Talon and Aggie's, but not until later.

The smell of pine was heavy in the air and when they got close enough to one, the smell of the little juniper trees was pungent and spicy. Bluebells and wild sunflowers were scattered along the bank and wild blueberries filled in wherever they could find space to grow. The air was warm and just slightly breezy. The river crashed by with enough force that it made hearing hard for conversation, and the trail was narrow and forced them to travel single file most of the time.

A blue jay landed in a tree a little ahead of them, and when they got to where it was, it flew just a little farther and waited again. Each time it landed it squawked a little and looked around like it wasn't watching them. Ducks, and now and then geese, flew up or down the river like they had all the time in the world to kill and were just enjoying a nice day. Lacey studied the water and once in a while she caught a flash of a salmon on its way to the headwater to spawn. It seemed a perfect day.

Louis took the lead and looked over his shoulder now and then to check on Lacey. He never got tired of looking at her. In fact, he worried about suffocating her with too much affection. But try as he might, he found it hard not to.

At one point, they rode close enough to the mountain that Lacey was able to reach out and pull a handful of sagebrush from one of the many on the riverbank. She put it to her nose and breathed deep. Since she was a child she had loved the smell of it.

In other places, she ran her hand along the face of massive flat-faced stones that grew thick green moss and bordered the edge of the trail. Heavy ponderosa pine with stumps three feet thick grew among the stones and dropped a blanket of long needles that covered the ground and got scattered onto the trail.

At times, she could hear the iron shoes of the horses on the rocks under them. Then, the sound would fade into the roar of the river and not be heard for long stretches at a time.

Louis had scouted the trail the day before and knew where he was headed. As they rounded the point of a bend in the river, a large flat rock protruded out into the water. It was about six feet above the water and they had to climb up onto it by way of smaller rocks that were set tight and could be trusted not to roll. The top of the rock was about six feet wide and ran flat as a table for about twenty-five or so feet. The water slammed into the upstream side of the rock like hitting a wall and pooled there before it washed around the end of it, and crashed on down the river. He had found the spot the day before and meant to return to fish salmon off it.

Today he had other plans. Lacey spread a small blanket on the rock and Louis handed her the basket with the food in it. They ate without saying much. It was enough to just be there. After they ate, they stood close to each other on the point of the rock and talked.

"I have a question," said Louis.

Lacey looked over at him. He wasn't much of a talker unless he was nervous. Then she had to race to keep up. She was ready for questions, if they were the ones she wanted. Namely, questions concerning marriage and things.

"It's about your menu," Louis continued. "It has a sort of riddle on the back. What does it mean?" He had memorized the words. "It says: Out of the root the rose bush grows, with thorns on its stem all the way to the rose. It's a riddle I think, but what does it mean?"

She was mildly disappointed that the question wasn't what she had hoped for. The fact that he had memorized the little ditty on the menu impressed her though. It meant that he liked her work. She did it a lot, and it was something she hoped he would appreciate.

Private time with Louis was rare and valued by Lacey. She found that she liked being close, and she was in a cuddly mood. She didn't mind making him wait for the answer. She took his hands in hers and put them behind her so that she was close enough to put her chin almost against his chest. It was a warm feeling. It was one of those things that never failed to make Louis smile. He always felt comfortable to her when he had that smile. She looked up into his strong grey eyes.

"Well," she said, "what do you see when you see a rose bush in the summer?"

"Roses," said Louis.

"Ya, me too," said Lacey, "but if you think of it, the bush has a lot more thorns than roses. We never notice them. We just look at the roses. That's Cougar Rock. I look down the street and see all the nice people and stores and I want to think that I'm seeing our little town. But our little town has more thorns than roses by far. Jeffery Baker for one, and he ain't the only one either. But maybe worse than that is the endless tunnels under our feet. It unnerves me to think that someone could be standing right under my feet at any time and I wouldn't know it, someone like Jeffery. Or maybe worse than that is that horrible hole in my hotel."

She fell silent for a bit.

"You mean the old cell?" Louis said.

"Ever been in there?" She asked him.

"Ya, it's pretty bad," said Louis.

"Bad don't even describe it, Louis." She got a disgusted look on her face and looked down at his chest. She had let go of his hands and had both her hands on his chest in front of her.

"I can't imagine how anyone could put someone in there and leave them. The only light they had was what little came in through the door. It smells like a grave in there. There are tobacco spit stains on the walls so thick that they ran down through all the desperate names that were left there and turned the dust black on the ground under them.

"It makes me think of someone trying to claw their way out of there and then giving up life and adding their name to the rest so they could lay down on that bug riddled bunk and die.

"And worse than that is that every time I pass by it, it feels like someone is watching me pass. Like they are hiding in there from Satan because they're pretty sure even he won't come in there after them. I've decided they would be right about that. Anyway, it is a constant haunt to me, and it stinks ten feet from the door. I hate that it's there. It gives me the creeps."

She was looking down, fiddling with one of the buttons on his shirt with both hands. Louis could see that she was genuinely upset, and it made him feel a little sad.

"Well," said Louis, "I might know a fella who could make that big black hole go away for you, for a small fee." She looked up at him. He was smiling.

"Oh ya," she said, "and how would he do that? Shovel it full of dirt one wheel barrel at a time?"

"No," said Louis, "I was thinking more along the lines of building a heavy pine door over the one that is there and putting a big lock on it. It would be flush with the wall and you wouldn't even notice it anymore. Also, it would smell like pine, much nicer."

That made her smile. "Well," said Lacey," I think I like your idea a lot."

She started looking a lot happier. Her famous Lacey smile had grown more sincere when she offered it to Louis. It was in her eyes, and he found it even more irresistible than before. She put her arms round him and cuddled closer. "So, just on the off chance that I would want this door, what would it cost me... if I'm willing to pay in kisses? Or would you demand cash? Don't know what I could afford to pay, in that case."

Louis was locked into the moment so tight that if a flash flood had suddenly happened he would be a quarter mile downstream before he realized it. He knew his face was getting a little red because he could feel it in his ears, but he didn't care. "Well," he said, "I've definitely been known to work for trade before, and I never heard of a better deal than kisses, but what are we talking here? I can make you a better deal if you pay in advance, you know."

Lacey giggled a little. It was a happy sound.

"Well tell me what the better deal looks like if I pay in advance. Would it be one, or two, or am I always going to be paying it off?" She had dropped a little hint she hoped he caught.

"Well, I'm thinking," said Louis, "that I should make two bids here. Now on the one offer, it would cost you one thousand kisses today and then you would be free of the debt, or you could pay only one today and five thousand more after we're married. I would definitely consider the last offer myself if I were you."

That was the offer she was hoping for and she could hardly contain herself. She was smiling so hard it almost hurt her face. "I think I like the last one myself," she said.

She was beside herself with joy. Louis was beaming, and his face was as red as the Indian paintbrush along the river. He knew she wanted to be with him, but hearing her say she would marry him was a dream he had not dared to dream. It was almost a spur of the moment thing.

He had wanted to ask Lacey but didn't have a clue how he should go about it. If she had said no, he would have wanted to leave town and never show his face again. Now he felt like the richest man in the country. He had seen how other men looked at Lacey, and being a man, he knew what most of them were thinking. But she was his now. He had been given a prize that he felt was more valuable then he deserved. He would see to it that she did not regret it.

The afternoon sun bounced off the reflections of the rapid water and the breeze caught Lacey's hair and shifted her dress as her face disappeared under the brim of Louis's hat. The little town of Cougar Rock made a change that would forever alter its history that day, and it all happened in that one brief moment. The day had been better then they could have hoped for, and they hated to leave Louis' fishing hole, but it was getting a little late and Lacey wanted to stop off at Talon's and Aggie's on the way back to town. More now, than ever. Now she had good news to tell.

They were forced to ride single file most of the way to the bridge and every time Lacey looked at Louis's back she smiled and felt good inside. It was evening before they got to Talon's and Aggie's. The sun was low in the sky and Talon heard them coming before he could see them. They were laughing and talking and laughing some more.

When the trail widened at the meadow they rode side by side so they could hold hands. Louis was a little sad that they had arrived and the rest of the ride would have to wait.

CHAPTER 20

HELL WAS CLOSER THAN SHE REALIZED

Talon recognized Lacey's voice and made for the house before they got there. He was standing on the balcony with Aggie and Reed when they rode up. The look on Lacey's face made Aggie smile. The only word she could think of was radiant. She looked radiant to Aggie.

"Hey," said Talon. "Good to see you guys. You just out for a ride, or was you planning to stop by?"

"You should stay for supper," Aggie called down from the balcony. "We have plenty."

"Wasn't planning to," said Louis, "but if Lacey wants to I suppose we can."

The conversation rattled on, and after supper Lacey helped Aggie clear the table. She was busting to tell someone about her engagement, and when they got into the kitchen she almost blurted it out without notice. The news soon spread to the rest of the house and the two couples were laughing and talking of it at a table on the balcony, when the subject of Jeffery came up.

"He was under your house?" said Lacey. "See what I mean by the thorns," she told Louis. She had a very matter of fact look on her face. "Are you sure it was him?" Lacey asked. She was genuinely concerned about people walking around under her feet without a sound.

"What did you do about it, anything?" She asked.

"Bought a dog," said Aggie.

The instant the words left her mouth Reed ran and got Shadow. It was the only part of the conservation he really understood. He held the fat puppy under its front legs and already its hind legs were dragging on the floor. "See," he said in a happy tone.

Lacey liked Shadow instantly. She hadn't expected a dog. She thought Talon might have tracked him down and set him straight on the rights of other people's privacy. But when she thought about it, a dog made the best sense. Anyway, Shadow had a friendly face, and Reed's smile always made her smile.

"He is beautiful," she said, "and he is already getting big." She reached to pet him.

"Ya," said Talon, "I think he might grow up to be a horse. Every pound of food seems to produce two pounds of puppy."

They all laughed a little and Lacey took Shadow in her arms. He tried to lick her face and put his feet on her shoulders and she had to eventually let Reed have him back.

"I wonder how he would do in the cave?" asked Lacey. "His nose should keep him from getting lost, don't you think?"

"I thought of that," said Talon, "so I tried him. He romped off up the little bench we once escaped from and crossed the vent hole we used without looking down. He jumped to the other side and disappeared into those teeth-like things that hang down. I let him go for a little and then tried to call him back. He don't do that very well yet and I thought I might have lost him.

"I wandered through those teeth up the shaft, and found where he used another smaller vent-like hole about the same size as the one we used. His tracks were in the bottom of it. It left the main shaft and I don't know where it went after that, but it took a long time before I saw him again.

I could hear him in there. He whined and I heard him run past in another shaft that must have a thin wall next to the one I was in, but I didn't want to try to follow him so I just kept calling him. He found his way back after about half an hour. I didn't try again. Maybe I will when he's a little older."

"How strange," said Lacey, "the caves are so close together you can hear from one to the other. I hadn't pictured that."

"They're not always that close," said Talon. "Most of the time there is a good distance between them. It seemed to me that they got more confusing, and we crossed more of them deeper into the mountain. You can't see much from our place but if you want, we can show you the one under us."

Lacey wasn't sure she wanted to. She hated the caves and the more Talon talked, the more she feared them. She agreed to go mostly because she hoped it would ease some of her anxiety about them. Also, there was Talon and Aggie. She wanted to understand what they were talking about when something cave-related came up. She looked a little nervous. "Well maybe," she said. "Is it safe?"

"I promise I won't leave you down there," said Talon. He smiled over at Louis. It seemed humorous to him that she was afraid to go even with other people into the cave. He knew that it really was a dangerous place but only to those who were desperate or dumb enough to go deeply into it.

The two couples went down the stairs to the iron door. Talon had gotten flashlights from Joseph the week before. The cave, so familiar to him, was amazing to Louis and Lacey. Louis kept flashing his light all over the walls and ceiling. They crossed the little stream and walked up to the small bench. From there they climbed up to what Talon had dubbed the lookout. It was above the little stream a good way, but the sound of the water was as easy to hear as it was on the cave floor.

From the little bench, they walked to the shallow trench that Talon and Aggie had escaped through. It was about five feet or so deep and cut across the shaft they were in below floor level. Talon explained how they crawled up for a long way before they came to the end of it, and he told of the stalactite that they wrestled onto the hole to plug it.

From there, he only remembered what the walls felt like. He explained the glass tubes and the sound of the great river. He also told of why his people were afraid of it and that he had family someplace in the mountain whose bones were forever entombed there.

The mountain is sacred he told them. The gold that is in there is the discovery of his people and should be left there, unless he or his people came for it, and could find it. After all, it is on Reservation land. That was a truth that most people either were not aware of or didn't care.

The story sent chills up Lacey's spine. She couldn't imagine being lost in a mountain of caves. But she decided, if she was, it would be Talon she would want to be lost with. She loved Louis, but Talon was literally part of the nature that built the cave and the mountain it was in. He was better equipped, she thought. They stood in the still depth of the cave, looking at the natural stone walls, and where there was flow rock, they studied the floor.

"Let me see your flashlight," Talon said to Louis. Louis thought the request was a little odd but he gave the light to Talon anyway. When Talon had both lights he shut them off.

"Oh," said Lacey. She sounded surprised. She stepped sideways until she felt herself bump into Louis. When she did she put her arm around his and took his hand. Even then she wasn't comfortable. The total absence of light was startling. She lifted her free hand and tried to see it. Without knowing it she touched her eyeball. It made her jerk her hand away and unnerved her. "Talon?" She said.

"I'm here," he said. "I wanted you to see what I mean by dark." His voice was lower than normal and his words seemed to echo off the walls in the distant cave. Lacey and Louis were without words.

"In this kind of dark," said Aggie, "I could walk away, and if you could not hear me you would not know I was gone until you tried to talk to me."

The thought of that made Lacey feel less secure than she already did. Aggie had not been in the cave since she and Talon had escaped it. It seemed long ago until she stood in the total absence of light and remembered. She remembered where she had heard Talon's voice, and quietly stepped over to him.

The wind in the distant cave moaned and blew past them, making it harder to hear Aggie's words. "When we were down here," she said, "one of the most important things was to never take a single step alone. We were tied together. If the bear found one of us he found us both."

Those words sank slowly into the minds of Lacey and Louis. Aggie took Talon's hand and put her hand up to his face. When she found his lips she crossed them with her index finger. Then she pulled gently on his arm and he slid his hand down the shaft past a stalactite and back the way they had come a few yards. While they were moving, Lacey was talking. She spoke loud enough to feel she was being heard over the sound of the cool damp wind.

"I can't imagine being lost in a place like this," Lacey said.

"You just wander like blind people," said Louis.

"What would you do if you came to a sudden drop?" Lacey asked.

Aggie's voice came from twenty feet behind them. "We did," she said, "more than once."

Lacey's heart skipped a beat. She nearly screamed a little, but was able to stifle it. Talon and Aggie were not beside her anymore. She started to panic a little. It was surprising how far they had gotten from her and Louis without leaving any hint of them leaving.

"Talon!" Lacey called out. Her voice sounded shaken and a little fearful.

When Talon heard the fear in her voice he turned one of the flashlights back on. He and Aggie were laughing at the joke. Louis laughed also, even though he told himself to remember not to give up the flashlight next time.

"How did you do that?" asked Lacey. She was genuinely amazed. "Ok, time to go!" Lacey said. She had hold of Louis's hand and Talon lit the way to where he was. By the time they got that far they were laughing themselves.

"That might be the most scary thing I ever did," said Lacey. She was laughing with relief that there was light again. It made her realize a little how it must have been for Talon and Aggie when they found their way out. Both couples laughed at the joke and they made talk of it all the way back out of the shaft through the iron door.

Once outside, Louis spread his arms in the last light of day and took a deep breath. They laughed at that, too. Talon remembered how it felt. It made him laugh out loud when he thought of Aggie's father and the look on his face on that evening.

Louis and Lacey held hands and laughed all the way back to town. Lacey kept trying to imagine how life would be once she was married. It felt scary and exciting at the same time. She looked over at Louis and even felt a little embarrassed. It occurred to her that she would one day soon take off her clothes in his presence, and he would do the same. That made her laugh again. The thought made her face turn red. She wondered if it wasn't the first time her face had ever turned red when she wasn't angry. She was normally not easy to embarrass.

Then she realized that things, for the first time in her life, were out of her control. She was going to hand over the head of house to Louis. He would be the final say. That bothered her and she looked over at him. He looked back and she shot him her famous Lacey smile.

He smiled and laughed a little. It reminded her a little of Shadow. Then she laughed a little too. *Ya right,* She told herself.

It had become a day she knew she could never match. She was so happy that she laughed out loud. Louis didn't know why, but he didn't care. He laughed because he was also feeling the joy and fear.

He wished that the moment would never end, and the road to town was his only destiny. He was enough of a realist to know that life would try to get even with them for the joy they felt and this might be the best day of his life. He soaked up every sparkle of Lacey's eyes and found them intoxicating and good.

Louis and Lacey got back to town a little after sunset. After they spent a few more minutes saying goodbye, they went home. Louis felt like singing, but he didn't. He knew he wouldn't sleep that night and he almost looked forward to it.

Chapter 21
Dealing With the Devil

Lacey sat at a table close to the door that led past the old jail cell and on to the back door. She was smiling, and silently writing sentences down on a piece of paper sack she got from the store. She began to lose the smile a little as she wrote. The thought of marrying Louis should have been the only thing on her mind. It wasn't. As soon as she was alone, she began to remember Jeff. He had the potential to destroy everything. If he decided to start talking to Louis, the right lies would be hard to expose.

She knew more now about the cave he wanted, but she also knew that it would be double-crossing Talon and Aggie if she told him. If she could be sure Jeff would only go there one time and then get lost, she would have felt much better. But she knew Jeff better than that. He was smart in spite of himself. He would try to learn the cave a little at a time. Even if he did get lost, it would take more than a time or two. Another thing that bothered her was the possibility of Jeff actually finding Talon's gold because she told him where to start looking.

She was lost in those thoughts when something caught her eye in the little mirrors that framed a painting she had just hung. She had replaced the mirror because it was cracked, and the crack was yellow. She stopped doodling to watch the small mirrors more closely.

At first, it was too dark in the back room to see what it was but it was moving closer. She kept her eyes fixed on the image. The mirrors were small, only about two inches square and she was sitting about ten feet away, but it wasn't long before she could see that it was a man's face.

He was behind her in the back room and had slipped up on her without her realizing it. At first she felt afraid. There should be no one in the back room. She realized that he had to have come in through the back door. She waited and watched the shadowy figure get closer.

She could feel her heart pounding and wished she was already married. Louis came to her mind. He would be able to handle any intruder. Even if this one only turned out to be a lost drunk, she wondered why the back door had not been locked. She would see to it that didn't happen again.

He was getting close enough to look over the swinging doors. As he moved into better view she could see who it was; it was Jeff. He was looking down at her from behind and hadn't realized that she knew he was there. Her face was aimed down but her eyes were looking up at the little mirrors.

"Well," said Lacey, "look what crawled in under the back door."

Jeff was a little surprised that she knew he was there. He hadn't made any sound he could detect and had not noticed the little mirrors. He pushed the swinging doors open and entered the main lobby. Then he pulled the chair out on the opposite side of the table from Lacey. He looked a little downcast and brought his eyes to rest on Lacey's face. He folded his arms and leaned back in the chair before he responded.

"I really don't know why you hate me so, Lacey. I would want to be your friend, even if I wasn't your father and the gold wasn't any part of this."

She knew that he knew why, and wasn't planning to start any "poor me" conversation with Jeff. She crossed her arms in front of her and stared back at him.

"Really Jeff," she said, "I wish you hadn't started talking just now. I was judging by the smell, and enjoying the thought that you might have died."

Jeff's clothes were dirty and his hair stuck out

from under his hat like oily strands of hair on a dead animal. He was also unshaven, and it looked like he had been for a while. He wore his hat pulled down and his hair was long enough that the bandana he wore pinned it to his sweat-streaked neck in the back.

The statement was pretty close to what Jeff was expecting. He was getting to know the newer, more grown-up version of Lacey Clanton.

"Well that isn't entirely my fault," said Jeff, "I don't have anyplace I can get a bath. The river is way too cold, and I don't have anything to heat water in, even if I wanted to. Besides that, it don't seem to bother my horse at all, so why bother."

He was trying to make a little joke. Lacey had heard Talon talk about that horse and when Jeff mentioned him she remembered what he had said.

"Well judging from how that horse looks," she said, "he probably can't smell. In fact, you might could convince me that he is about dead himself. How did you get in through the back door?" She wanted to know.

"Not locked," said Jeff. "Anyway, what would you like me to do. It don't seem you want people knowing anything, so I thought it best not to come in through the front, where anyone could see how often I have to do it. You could get rid of me quick if you would just loosen up a little and find out what I need to know."

Lacey thought about what Jeff was saying. She wasn't ready to give up any information yet, if she ever would be. Still, she knew that he was right about not coming in through the front door. She hadn't figured a way to get rid of him yet, and until she did she needed to keep him under wraps.

For the moment, that was not something she had figured out well either. She had some eyes on Jeff but only when he was available. He was a natural sneak, and hard to keep an eye on. She remembered how he seemed to always know when Ed was gone so he could sneak in and visit her mother. It made her wonder if he wasn't somehow the reason Ed always believed that his neighbors were out to get him.

"What do you want from me?" She asked. "I told you I don't know anything. Why do you think Talon would tell me where that gold is?"

"You're his friend," said Jeff. "You was at his house tonight. You could have asked him. I think you might want to help me, Lacey. If you value that friendship you might. I don't care what it takes, Lacey. I don't mind doing what I have to do to get in there.

"As much faith as you put in that Indian and the smithy, they're both at my mercy. Anything burns, especially if it's made out of nice dry pine. I could easily leave your smithy digging his anvil out of the ashes, and your Indian too."

The thought of that made Lacey's blood run cold. She instantly thought of the hotel fire. Her eyes widened, and her features stiffened a little.

"Why do you think I wouldn't tell the sheriff if you tried something that evil?"

"I would think you might be smarter than that," said Jeff. "All I would need to do is say you helped me do the whole thing. After all you bought the hotel, and shall we mention how you got such a good deal on it?"

She realized he was right again. He had all his ducks in a row. That didn't surprise her. She was getting used to it. She knew he wasn't bluffing. He couldn't have known she was going to buy the hotel or even that she wasn't still in Wolf Creek at the time he set the fire. So why did he set it? She hadn't heard of anything to do with insurance and it made her wonder.

He all but admitted that he had done it. But what good was that? He had thought it all through. He had her over a barrel. She needed some leverage over him. At this point, she couldn't chance being implicated in his evil. Even if she found a way to get some sort of proof that Jeff had started the fire to the sheriff, Jeff might still bring her down with him. A strong case could easily be made against her, and even if nothing could be proven it would ruin her reputation with everyone.

Now on top of everything else, he was threatening Louis too. Talon or Louis could turn him inside out and shake his bones free of his hide like a rug. That is, if he was man enough to face them. That's when she realized why he came so late to see her. Louis was in his way.

"You followed us?" Lacey asked.

"Nope," he said. "Didn't need to. Saw you coming from Talon's house."

"Then you were spying on Talon," Lacey said. "Even a snake has enough grit to face a man."

She was incensed that he was always stalking everyone. It wasn't bad enough that the caves were always there. Besides that, he was above ground watching every move she made.

She glared at him from across the table. He had left her in a helpless place. At first it made her want to cry in frustration and anger, but she refused. She wanted to kill him, but she wasn't sure how she could go about it or if she could do it. She decided she needed time to try to figure a way out of the mess she found herself in.

"I don't know when I will see Talon and Aggie

again. When I do, I will try to learn what I can. Until then, you stay out of here. Don't come around me or any of my people, or I swear to God I will kill you, and if I hang, I hang."

She was trembling with anger and Jeff knew she meant it. He didn't care, she was finally cracking and soon he would have what he wanted. If he could just find where Talon had gone when he left his shaft, and what the rest of the trip in the cave seemed like to him, it would give him a direction. He was smart enough to realize that the cave system was far too complex to try without knowing something. He had almost been lost forever already. If she could just steer him in the right direction, he could do the rest. He had the best lights money could buy. There had to be tracks left in the cave and no one could go that long without urinating. There would be evidence to follow if he could just find what shaft they used when they left.

He knew he would only get one try. Once he left Talon's cave he would be on his own and couldn't risk coming back that way unless he had enough gold to make it worthwhile.

He thought of just going on Sundays when Talon and Aggie would be in church, but he knew that Talon would know and lay in wait for him after the first time he tried it. He had exhausted every idea he could think of for getting into the cave safely. In the best of conditions the cave might still kill him, but without that gold he didn't think he had much to look forward to anyway.

The hike to where Talon's cave was took a long time and was still too risky. That he could deal with now, but Talon was another thing. He was convinced that Talon would shoot to kill if he found him under his house. He also needed to know what to look for after leaving Talon's part of the cave.

He thought of finding another vise, something that would force the information out of the people who had it. Lacey might come through, but a little backup plan couldn't hurt. He decided that a little research was in order, and when he got the chance he would need to spend a little time at the court-house. Anyway, he had a little time to kill while he waited. He figured he would use a some of it on re-search. Research had gotten him a lot of good infor-mation in the insurance business. He knew Lacey could only hold out for so long. Sooner or later she would have to actually talk to Talon. All he needed to do was keep up the pressure.

Louis was another problem. Jeff knew that he would smile while he beat him to death and that he likely could. The only hope he held on that front was the boot pistol. He would just come and go late and hope that he could avoid Louis.

Lacey followed Jeff to the back door and watched him leave. When she went to lock it after him the key turned in the lock but she pulled the door to be sure, and it came open. She instantly knew Jeff had done something. She opened the door and looked at the strike plate. Someone had filled it with clay. The door wasn't able to latch. The clay was a nice light blue color. It was natural clay and had a little sand in it.

She wondered when Jeff had found time to do that. The door was usually locked. He must have been watching the door for hours. She shook her head, and started to dig the clay out but thought better of it. Letting him use it would keep him from finding some other way she wouldn't know about, and this way he could come in without being seen. It was better for the moment.

She hated everything about Jeff. She especially hated that he was her father. It made her feel bad for Ed, and herself as well. Ed would not have done things any different, but that didn't change how it made her feel.

Talking to Jeff, she knew what he said was true. It would look like they came at the same time and were together. That was made worse by the fact that he had set the hotel fire. It not only made her look guilty of stealing the hotel but it implicated her in whatever else he was into.

She wondered what he held over her mother, if anything, that would cause her to want him around.

She figured he told her he would expose who he was to Ed. All that was past for now. She was in deep and hated herself for keeping so much from the people she loved in order to cover things up. Jeff held the power to destroy the lives of everyone she knew and loved.

For now she was caught, and the only way out was through Jeff. She needed to get rid of him, either in the cave or through the law. But if Jeff knew she had turned him in to the law he would be more dangerous than ever. She had no way to prove they had not made plans for the hotel in advance.

She wondered how things had gone so wrong, as she went up to her room. She had made an honest start and was doing better than she could have ever dreamed. Now it was all messed up, and there was no way to keep it from ending poorly.

Even if she told him what she now knew of the cave, she would be turning her back on Talon. If she waited she might lose Louis and Talon. What good would the hotel be then? Nothing would matter and

Jeff would likely walk away like he always had. He was the ultimate weasel and so far no one had ever been able to catch him. She threw herself onto her bed and cried herself to sleep.

CHAPTER 22

CIRCLE OF DEATH

Jeff had left his horse grazing on the grass in the cemetery. When he left the hotel, he headed back that way through the trees a little way off the road. He found his horse and rolled out his bedroll a little way from where he was grazing.

The morning showed up before the sun actually rose. The sky was clear, and Jeff was awakened by coyotes howling only a few hundred feet from where he had slept. Songbirds started chirping and a finch darted from one tree to another not far away. He lay and listened for a little. It helped him know if he was alone.

He heard geese come up the river and in a little while sandhills flew overhead and called down to the earth with their odd-sounding voices, almost like pigeons make but nicer to hear. It seemed early in the year for them to be migrating, but maybe they were just hanging around like all the other birds.

He liked the morning. Morning was easier, the nights were getting worse. He was having trouble falling asleep, and he worried that if something didn't change, the weather would eventually drive him into the shaft for shelter. He tried sleeping in the cave a couple times, but it made little noises that he didn't recognize and kept him awake too much. It seemed something was always moving down there.

During the day, however, it had become a hiding place and he had wandered around in it as far as he dared, looking for gold or just looking. He dragged a small dead Juniper tree over to the hole. He had it stowed in a hollow not far from where he kept his horse. He had cut off the limbs so that they were only about six-or-so inches long.

It made a usable ladder that no one would readily recognize as a ladder.

He was about to drop it into the hole but Seth already had his ladder in the way. It was early, way too early for Seth to be in the shaft. He had never done that before. It puzzled Jeff. He didn't like surprises. He didn't like company either, but there wasn't much he could do about Seth.

He dropped his ladder into the hole and used Seth's ladder to climb down on. Then he dragged his little tree far enough into the shaft to conceal it and left it by the wall where he had the rest of his stuff stashed. From there he knew the cave well. He had a pan and kept it with him in case anyone ever questioned why he was there, if anyone ever came onto him in the cave. He liked to have all his bases covered.

He walked silently into the shaft and took the first right. That shaft went on to a confusing trick of the cave that nearly got him once. After a bit of a hike, he left that shaft and entered one that was not much more than a crack in the wall. It started small-er and grew to about ten feet high in a little while. He started a small climb and could hear the water-fall he had climbed on his way to Talon's. It was straight ahead.

The little stream hadn't interested him in the past but the noise was what he liked about it now. It created a sort of sound closet he felt safer in. He had followed it downstream one day. It flowed parallel to the shaft he had just used. It was odd that it didn't just flow right down it. The route it took was only a few inches lower. It flowed in a semi-circle about a hundred feet around and then came to a place where it ran into large ceiling rock that was on the floor. It was piled like rip-rap, and the little stream disap-peared into it. The rip-rap looked like the shaft had caved in and the cave ended there.

He wasn't headed to Talon's today. Today he was just killing time. Lacey needed time to think about what he had told her and if she was smart, go get the information he needed.

He had grown tired of eating salmon and the run seemed to be thinning a little anyway. He was hungry and broke and feeling a little weak. He walked up to the little fall and sat down. The water was only a small stream about eight feet wide and, in most places four to six inches deep, and it didn't actually fall. It just dropped so rapidly that it was more like a fall than a normal rapid. He discovered he could climb it with ease with his boots off.

He sat down and turned off his light to rest. The air was cool and damp and a great relief from the Idaho heat that would soon soak the earth outside. He was almost asleep when he saw movement from the corner of his eye.

It was a dim light. Someone was in the cave and had gotten to the falls from a shaft that joined his at a weird angle. It entered about three feet off the floor, and just behind him. He took it for some sort of natural vent, and Jeff had never explored it. It was a small shaft and he wasn't interested in it. Someone was though, and they were headed his way. He decided to turn on his light and look busy. He scooped up a little gravel and sand near the bank of the little stream and turned his back on the intruder while he washed it.

Seth had been in the cave all night. He went in to keep tabs on the water under the hotel. It was a constant worry to him that someone might go in there and do something stupid like urinate in it. He also worried about rats and mice getting in, now that the hole was open. A dead animal in the bath water would not be good for business.

He had left a couple of batteries in the cave by the hole in case he got all the way down there and ran out. He got the idea of exploring more of the cave when he saw that someone had been using the grave-hole to come and go.

Jeff had left tracks in the dirt outside the hole, and a few inside that were in trackable soil. Seth figured it was Jeff because he had seen him around the cemetery. No one else came there much. Even Jeff only came when he thought Seth was gone.

The first thing Seth saw was Jeff's stash as he rounded the bend from the hole and started down the shaft. The next thing he saw was curious to him. Someone had marked the wall of the shaft on either side with chalk. There were arrows pointing out of the cave all the way. That gave him a false sense of security. He assumed that he could follow the arrows in and out without any trouble. He found that he was wrong. He had the extra batteries from the stash at the hot spring and that too let him think he was good to go.

He had been in the cave following the arrows and exploring for about four hours. Now and then another shaft came and went but as long as he stayed his course he always found more arrows on the wall.

In the course of time, he spotted something he found disturbing. There was an arrow that had a slash through it. He thought he had seen it before. The slash was small but obvious once he noticed it. He was sure he had seen others like it but he hadn't paid enough attention to know where. He stood for a moment and looked around.

His first set of batteries were getting weak, so he took the opportunity to change them. He knelt down so as not to lose any part of the light in the process. When he was finished he started to stand again but in the beam of the light he noticed human tracks in the dusty sand of the floor. He stared at them for a second and suddenly realized that some of them were his. He had been here at least two other times. The arrows must go in a circle, he thought.

After his discovery, he took note of every step he took. Other shafts and small trickles of water became potential landmarks. He began to realize that one of the shafts that either crossed or joined his was how he came in. The marks were only on the walls between the other shafts and only then where the walls had a flat place smooth enough to leave a good mark.

The shaft he was in was a circle. He was walking past the shaft he needed to get out. The arrows must have been too far back in the exit shaft to notice them. As he worked his way around the same giant circle, he tried to remember anything that he saw so that if he saw it again he would know. Then he remembered what started him knowing. It was the little slash on the arrow. It must mean something. He watched for and found it hours later. The new batteries were getting weak by then like the others.

He, like Jeff, had left the old ones on the floor and he noticed them first. He was tired and almost in a panic before he came to them. When he did he stopped and looked around the shaft. At first, all he saw were the walls of the shaft. So he walked back a few yards. Going the other way he found a shaft that entered his at a steep angle. Down that shaft, he found more arrows. It had to be the right one. He had walked past it again.

If he had not turned around he would have never found it. It was just a dark place in the wall like all the others going the way of the arrows. Down that shaft, he found a place where the floor had good loose dirt and found that he could see his tracks again but only one set. There were also Jeff's tracks but he wore different boots.

He was starting to worry that he would not have enough light to find his way out. His light was getting so weak that he was finding it hard to see the arrows. He wished he had kept the old batteries. They might have a little life left in them, and he might need it.

Another shaft appeared and he passed it. Too many of the cave shafts he found were only like a dent in the wall. They only went a few yards and ended. That made it easy to overlook a real shaft.

A while later the one he was in was getting smaller. He could not remember crawling any place on his way in, but he was beginning to see that if he continued on he might have to crawl to get through. A short time later it closed up until he was crawling.

He tried to find more arrows but there were none that he could see in the dim light. He stayed in the shaft until he was on his hands and knees all the time. It was the wrong way he knew, but he was too tired to go back. He thought about it and decided to rest a while and maybe sleep. His light was almost gone but if he rested he would go back anyway and try to find where he went wrong.

He sat back against the wall and closed his eyes. The light was off. He hoped it would somehow help the batteries. When he relaxed, his heart stopped pounding and he realized he could hear water falling. It seemed close, so he turned the light back on and crawled a little farther. By sheer luck, he had left the main shaft into another one that intersected with Jeff's waterfall.

Chapter 23

A Dark Dusty Hole

Jeff had turned his light on and it was brighter and much bigger. He had ordered his from the big city and picked it up in Bear Valley. It was cutting-edge technology for the day and used four batteries at a time. It was designed for a floodlight and lit the whole shaft like day when he turned it on. Seth saw it come on as he moved forward. For a moment he thought he might have somehow found daylight. He crawled to the opening and stared out at Jeff and the waterfall.

The light was reflecting off the water as it cascaded down the steep slope behind Jeff. That sent little mirror-like reflections all the way down the shaft. It was a little mesmerizing at first and he just sat and looked.

He thought it odd that Jeff hadn't noticed him yet but reasoned that his light was too dim and the bigger light drowned it out.

"Hello," said Seth.

He was so relieved to see Jeff that he didn't even try to actually see who it was. He thought it must be Jeff. He hadn't seen anyone else ever hang around the cemetery. He hadn't seen Jeff up close before, but that was his best guess.

Jeff turned around trying to look surprised. He hadn't expected Seth to wander over into his side of the hole. And he was a little surprised to see that he had. He normally stayed on the side with the hot spring.

"Well look who dropped in," said Jeff. "You lost?"

"If this ain't the West Branch Hotel I am," said Seth, "and it don't look much like it." He was feeling very relieved that he had found anyone who could show him the way back to the hole. He slid out of the little vent he was in and walked over to where Jeff was squatting. He held out his hand to shake.

"Sure glad you are here," Seth said, "I was running out of light."

"Jeff was glad to see it was only Seth. He worried that another miner or even Axle Ford might be looking for him.

"What happened?" Jeff asked. "You look whipped. Been lost a while have ya?"

"Seems like a long time," said Seth, "I came in and got a little too curious I guess. That was in the afternoon. I think I've been in here all night, maybe. You don't know what time it is, do ya?"

"It's early," said Jeff, "must be about seven or eight or so. You maybe should go find breakfast and a bed pretty soon."

Breakfast sounded good to Seth. He suddenly felt he could eat for a week. Truthfully, he felt that way most of the time, but more so now.

"Ya and about a half gallon of coffee to boot," said Seth. He was smiling. He had a perpetual, wide smile that made his white teeth look even whiter, and he always looked as if he was about to break out laughing. It usually had a positive effect on people. Even Jeff found himself smiling back.

"Well," said Jeff, "always good to see a neighbor drop by. You find anything interesting while you were wandering around in there?" He wasn't sure what else to say. He wanted any information he could get about the cave system and wondered how far Seth had wandered.

"Not much," said Seth. "I found a lot of chalk lines though. First, they got me lost, then they got me found again."

Jeff laughed a little. "Sounds familiar," he said, "I got a little lost putting them there."

Seth wanted to get out of the cave and on his wa,y but he also wanted to know more about Jeff. Jeff was washing the sand he had scooped up and trying to think of a way to get any information about the hotel and Lacey. He also wanted to create good relations with Seth. He figured it might be useful in times to come.

Seth was doing a little fishing of his own. He didn't really care that Jeff was in the cave but he knew Lacey didn't like him. "Well I'm sure glad you did it," he said, "or else I might still be in there. How much of the cave did you mark? Is there more of it you found? I went on what was a big circle, but is there more to see that you marked?"

People as private as Jeff were questionable to him. Besides that, the cave was interesting especially if all the stories about gold were true. He had often wondered what lay beyond the hot spring, but the passage around the spring was narrow and slick. One fall could result in being all but boiled to death. He didn't want to know that bad.

"No, not much," said Jeff. "It's a big system and dangerous. Kinda decided this was far enough in for me." He didn't want to tell Seth that if he climbed the waterfall he would find more arrows and if he understood the slash marks and the words with them he could eventually get all the way to Talon's. He had marked the shafts he found with a "no" or a "U" for unknown. He used the slashes to tell him that he was coming to a place where he needed to make a sharp turn. The number of options were not that many, but they went long distances, and he had given up on some if he decided they had gone too far to get him to Talon's cave.

The problem was, every time he tried to come back, he would get a little confused. Even if there were only a few choices, the threat remained that he might have walked into the one he was in without noticing and the one he was looking at might be where he came from, or not.

Another problem, was that where he found sections of the oldest part of the system there was what looked like marble or quartz that appeared to have flowed out of nowhere and made the floor and walls impossible to mark. It was a milky color and had grey or green streaks in it like they had been dripped onto it and flowed with the rock. It was smooth and beautiful to look at. It was also dangerous. In those places, there were usually stalagmites and stalactites that made it hard or impossible to see any distance ahead and also couldn't be marked.

An intersecting shaft in such a place could easily be overlooked if it happened on the opposite side of a stalactite, or if the stalactite was big enough, and some were, even a stalagmite could let a small vent of shaft go unnoticed until he was coming down the shaft on that side on a return.

He had found his way to Talon's only because the shaft that finally got him there was a lava tube that ran uninterrupted for almost three miles and only had one other shaft that crossed it near its end. The lava tubes held a little mystery for him.

He had ridden around an amazing lava flow south and east of Boise that was on the surface. It flowed just like water that had been made of rock. Strange shapes had formed in it and a very colorful cinder had formed that he picked up and kept a little of. It glistened in the sun with rainbow colors that he found interesting. He wondered why the shafts never had any of them. They were obviously caused by lava.

He had discovered a lot of lava tubes in the caves and marked most of them, as well as the more interesting shafts that he thought to be older. The information he had left led to Talon's cave. He had no intention of offering that information up to anyone.

Seth looked around the shaft. It was amazing to him that there could be running water underground. The hot spring was like a little lake, not flowing. He wondered if it leaked in from the Clearwater somehow. He stood for a moment looking at Jeff, not sure what he should do next.

"I suppose..." said Jeff. He was moving a little sand in the last of the pan wash with his fingers. He stopped talking in mid-sentence. He lifted the pan a little higher and tipped it to the light. Then he smiled and put the tip of his finger into the edge of the pan. There was gold, not a lot but enough to scoop up a little with his fingertip. Seth could see that he was genuinely surprised. He was standing a little to the left of Jeff.

"You getting rich?" Seth asked.

"Not yet," said Jeff.

He almost said how surprised he was and then remembered that he wanted everyone to think he had been working the claim all along. "I'll just add it to the rest," he said, "If I live long enough I might."

"Well good luck on that," said Seth. "I'm not going to live long enough to see the sun set if I don't get food soon."

"I hear that," said Jeff. "Just head straight out this shaft until you get to the end. It will dump you into another one. Go left and left again. As soon as you come around the corner you'll see the light."

Seth thanked him and walked right out in a few hundred yards or so. As he rounded the corner he saw how he missed the shaft the first time. He had seen the arrows on the left and walked right past the shaft Jeff was in. Another fifty feet later he saw Jeff's stash again and walked by it. He noticed that Jeff had a special belt that looked like a bullet belt only it had loops large enough to hold batteries for his big light, maybe twenty or so.

Talon watched Seth leave from the top of the waterfall. He was standing just far enough back so that all that was exposed to the bottom of the fall was his head.

He had found Jeff's marks easy to follow. Shadow, the night before, had seemed uneasy and whined as he paced the floor. Talon got up and let him out for a little. When he came back in he sat and looked out over the balcony without returning to his place by the stove. It was enough to make Talon uneasy. He gathered his 38 Smith and Wesson and all the batteries he could put in his pockets for the flashlight and crept down the stairs to the iron door.

Once in the cave he stood and listened for a long time in the dark. When he was sure he was alone he walked through the cave to the place where he had found the hole in the ceiling.

He hadn't planned on ever going farther, but Shadow got him thinking. Without knowing how Jeff got in, he had no way of protecting his family. He told himself he wouldn't go far. Not knowing made him feel too vulnerable. It was something he needed to do for his own sanity. He decided to find out how Jeff had gotten into his shaft, and if possible find a way to stop him. Now he knew; it was not good news. He watched until Seth's dim light faded out down the shaft and then stepped back and returned home.

Chapter 24

Snoop Versus Snoop

Once out of the hole, Seth made a beeline for the hotel. It was pushing eleven in the morning by the time he got a bath and came in. Lacey saw him come in and wasn't busy, so she went over to his table right away.

"Mornin Seth," she said. "What do ya know?"

Seth was smiling as usual. He had his arms folded over his chest. He had on a new blue shirt and clean pants. He had left a new hat he just bought in his room. It had gotten dirty in the cave and he wanted to look good. He had news.

Lacey could see he was feeling proud about something.

"I was right," he said. "It was Jeff. He has the cave marked a long way in with chalk. Don't try to follow it. Nearly got me killed. I found him in there. He was panning at a little fall of water he found, but he hadn't been panning in it before. He had no work done around the stream, like gravel piles, and he had no place to dry gold set apart either. All he had was one pan. He did find a little gold, but it surprised him more than it did me. It looked like he has been climbing the little fall and using the cave it flows from.

"He kept himself between me and the falls, anytime he could. And, he was a little too careful about how much he said about how much of the cave he has marked. Who knows where he has been?

"His marks are hard to figure until you realize that he was kinda lost himself when he made them. That ain't all. He has a belt like a bullet belt, but for batteries. They go to a flashlight bright enough to outshine the sun. I ain't never seen such a light. He stowed a pile of things right close to the hole. Anyway, I doubt he has been mining, but I bet he will be now."

That wasn't great news for Lacey. It meant Jeff wouldn't be leaving even if she could think of some way to get him to lose interest in Talon's gold. She had hoped she could starve him out, but not now. It did confirm what she already suspected. Jeff had been using the grave hole to access Talon's cave. At least now she knew where to find him if she needed to.

Aggie woke almost as soon as Talon left. She was on the landing when he got back. She had been out there most of the night. It was pushing noon when he closed the iron door again and climbed the stairs. Aggie had discovered the door open and knew he had gone into the cave. She followed far enough to find that he was not in the shaft under the house. When he didn't come back, the panic she already felt continued to grow. She had been praying and crying. She knew he was wise enough to know what he was doing, but she also knew the cave.

Talon found her on the landing. Her face was tear-streaked, and she had not eaten. The kitchen was cold. He knew why, and it made him sorry he hadn't woken her up. She was so relieved to see him that she wanted to fly into his arms and cry more. She heard the iron door when it closed and thanked Jesus in heaven that he had come home. Then she began to heat up. She had worried for nothing.

"You promised!" she spat. By now, what she wanted to do was scream in his face. But she had learned how to make him regret without disrespecting his position as the head of her house. She wasn't sure she wanted him to regret, but she meant to find out. She waited to hear what he had to say first.

"I know I did. I'm sorry. I wasn't planning to go

so far. I found marks on the cave wall. They go all the way to town."

"You snuck out," she said.

He could see that she wanted to fly into his face like an ice storm. With the worry of the moment, he had forgotten time. There was no way to keep track of it while he was in the cave. He knew he had been gone a long time, but it surprised him how long. He kept telling himself he would be back just a little late for breakfast. She wouldn't have time to worry too much.

"Shadow woke me up," he said. "He seemed to know something. I checked the shaft and found nothing, but it was time to at least look into how Jeff got in. You are not safe as long as he can come and go under us. He could try anything. I really needed to know."

"You promised not to go alone," she said. "I hope it was worth it."

"Well," said Talon, "I think it was. A child could find our place the way he has it marked up. I really didn't take any chances. It was like following a stream. I wouldn't have taken even the smallest risk of getting lost. Still, I should have woken you up. I thought I could get back a lot sooner. Sorry."

He really did feel sorry for Aggie, but he was glad he went. Aggie could see the hurt in his eyes and remembered that he loved her. When she looked into his eyes, she almost felt bad for being angry. Talon knew he had said all he could. He had made a decision, and he meant to end the Jeff Baker problem. "We need to go into town," he said, "I need dynamite."

Aggie forgot everything about her worry and waiting instantly. He said it like it was an everyday event that he would want, of all things, dynamite. "Dynamite?" she said. "What on earth for? You could kill yourself. Do you even know how to use dynamite? You could bring down half the mountain, Talon."

"I don't need a lot," Talon said, "just enough to close the shaft between us and the rest of the cave on the river side to the mountain."

The thought of Talon using dynamite would have frightened her if he were only planning to play with it outside. When she realized what he wanted it for, it terrified her.

"Talon," she said, "I don't think dynamite is a very good idea. Can't you find another way to stop people from getting in? An explosion in the cave could have very bad results."

She could see she was talking to a wall. He had set his jaw and she knew that was that. Her last hope was prayer. It hadn't failed her yet. She got up and set about fixing something for the family to eat.

Axle Ford was having lunch with Domingo in the office. Seth had brought it to them. Seth didn't need the money he earned working for Lacey anymore, but he liked her. In fact, what he felt might be more like love. He watched her when she wasn't looking, and knew more about her moods than some men might ever learn.

She was more beautiful than anyone he had ever known. Just being close to her made him feel special. His experience in life had been just the opposite of acceptance. She made him feel privileged to be there. Domingo gave him two bits every time he brought them lunch. That too, made him feel a part of the people of the town. He was becoming well-liked and well known.

"You get any reply from Boise yet?" Domingo asked Axle.

"Ya," said Axle, "I forgot to tell you. Came in couple days ago. You were right, Brogan 'was' wanted in Boise. That's the reason I forgot to mention it. Been workin on it. He had help there. Someone would vandalize a piece of property. Brogan would use the damage for his example. "That someone was never seen, but the sheriff there is certain that he existed. They were watching Brogan close enough to know where he was when a new event happened.

Anyone who didn't buy would soon after have problems with the accomplice. Things must have gotten hot and they came here."

"No idea who?" Domingo asked.

"Yep," said Axle. "Thought at first it might be Lacey Clanton. She arrived right after the fire. That's about the same time Jeff Baker did. There is some kind of connection there, but I can't find it. I checked though, just to see.

According to what I can learn from the telegraph office, she traveled alone. There is a stage stop about halfway tween Wolf Creek and Billings where she spent the night. The waiter had no trouble remembering her at all. Said she pulled a gun on him."

"Pulled a gun? Did he say why?"

"Said he wasn't sure. From what she told him, it seemed he didn't bring her coffee fast enough. I figured I must have missed something. Who would pull a gun on a waiter for not being more prompt with their coffee?"

"Oh I don't know," said Domingo, "I have days like that now and then." He was smiling and Axle smiled a little too.

"Ya, I can picture him like he is now, packing that pot with him everywhere he goes." Both men laughed at the thought.

"Anyway, said Axle, "she arrived alone and no one followed after her when she left. Your old boss in Billings said she was alone there as well. I don't think she would be involved with a rat like Jeff anyway.

"Seems the bank in Wolf Creek can vouch for her money coming from her father Ed Clanton when he sold out. Your old boss said she was looking for a bank in Billings. The bank there said she had a good sum of cash, wouldn't say how much. She wanted a cashier's check for it. They gave it to her. That raised the hair on my neck a little but I don't think it was anything. We could ask her but I don't really think we need to.

"She was still in Wolf Creek when the Brogan team was in Boise. It did look good for a while though. She got here at the perfect time and bought the hotel right after the fire. But no way she could have been the accomplice. It's Baker, I'm completely convinced of it."

"Good enough for me," said Domingo. "How do we nail him?"

"For now, we wait," said Axle. "We got all the circumstantial evidence we need. Nothing solid yet. That's coming though. All we can do is keep watching and wait. He will let us know when it's time to hang him, they always do."

Domingo knew Axle was right. He had yet to fail to get to the bottom of things. He trusted Axle for a lot of things. Getting information was the thing he was best at.

CHAPTER 25

CHALK MARK THAT

Talon and Aggie rode into town with the wagon. Aggie didn't want to go with him to the General Store to buy the dynamite. He left her at the West Branch and rode on alone. He didn't really want to use dynamite, but he couldn't think of another way. It would have to do.

The street was busy when they arrived. The crows were keeping their tireless watch over Main Street from the tops of any structure tall enough to interest them. Another dog had begun to hang around the saloon. He was a big yellow lab-cross that one of the miners owned. He wasn't quite as lazy as the other two, and could usually be seen sitting on the boardwalk not far from the door. He had wandered up the street and watched Talon pull up to the hitching post in front of the General Store.

A wide-faced, rather thin old man with hooded eyes and red hair rode a stout-looking horse past. He was wearing homespun pants that looked like they hadn't been washed since they were made. His worn out cotton top that he wore for a shirt had holes in the elbows and cigarette burns on the chest and belly. It was the color of a cloudy day but it could be seen that it was once white. He called to the dog, who trotted off behind him as he rode on down the street.

The old miner had a brown hat that had a wide brim that had never been blocked and was old. He smiled at Talon as he went by. Talon smiled back and waved. The old man's hat made Talon smile. It reminded him of the one Seth used to have.

Talon bought six sticks of forty percent dynamite

from Joseph, who was a little concerned about selling it to him. He knew Talon well enough to know he wasn't a hard rock miner, but figured it none of his business and let him have it.

Talon paid and headed back for the hotel. Louis was there having lunch with Lacey. They were sitting at a table with Aggie and Reed. Reed had a fresh cookie and a glass of soda. He hardly noticed when Talon came in. He did glance out the window to be sure his dad hadn't somehow lost Shadow. He was sitting on the seat where Talon sat to drive the horses.

Reed raised his arm as high as he could and waved at Shadow. Aggie smiled when she saw him do it. She was glad to see Talon. Knowing he had bought the dynamite gave her an odd feeling, like he had just shot the neighbor's dog or something. Justified or not, it just didn't seem like a good idea to her. She was glad Louis was there. She had a plan to get him to help Talon with the dynamite.

"Did you get it?" Aggie asked Talon.

"I got it," he said.

"You could get someone who knows more about it, you know."

She was looking at Louis when she spoke. Talon knew the cat was out of the bag and would have not mentioned it otherwise.

"You any good with blowing up mountains?" Talon asked Louis.

Louis smiled. He didn't know what Talon was talking about but it sounded fun. "How many mountains you want to blow up?" Louis asked

"Just one," Talon told him. "I just bought six sticks of dynamite at the store and I want to blow a shaft closed with it."

Louis raised his eyebrows and smiled. "Never used the stuff myself, but I know who has. Let's ask Dexter. He knows."

That sounded like a good idea to Talon, and after lunch the two men walked back to the Anvil. Dexter was a little busy, but he stopped to listen to the two men. Talon told him what he had and what he want-ed to do with it.

"How much powder you buy?" Dexter asked.

Talon guessed at what he meant by powder. "Six sticks of forty percent."

"Six sticks?" Said Dexter. "Forty percent? You could level half the Sawtooth Mountains with that much nitro. Why so much?"

"Well," said Talon, "I didn't know, so I just got what I figured was enough. Saw some that was less percent but didn't know how much I needed. Won't get more than one try at it."

Dexter thought on it and decided that if he wanted his friends alive he better go along for the ride. "Okay I'll go," he said, "but you need to take four of them sticks back to the store. If we need more an two, it's too big a job for me. You get any fuse?"

"Fuse," said Talon. He had forgotten fuse.

"Well," said Dexter, "you can't set it off by willing a curse against it. Get enough to be clear a good way before it blows. Get a couple blasting caps too."

On the way back to the hotel, they got the fuse and caps. Talon was already feeling good about closing the shaft. If someone wanted to visit his house they could come to the front door like everyone else.

Talon tied the top of the flour sack Joseph gave him with the fuse in it, and went into the hotel. Lacey and Aggie were having coffee and pie. He sat down and had coffee with them. As the two women talked, Talon and Reed sat and listened. Reed seemed to like watching the people who came and went and paid close attention when they paid. It was a curious thing to him.

Talon saw that there were a few pieces of paper on the table and out of boredom picked up one of them. It had writing on the back of it. He could make out some of the words but not all of them. He looked over at Louis and wanted to ask, but was a little embarrassed that he couldn't make it out on his own.

When Lacey left to go for more coffee, he handed it to Aggie to read. She could see what he wanted and read it out loud: "Under the flowers in the yard by the street, go the shadowless plodding of an enemy's feet." She looked up at Talon and put the paper back on the table. No one needed an explanation.

The three men met at Talon and Aggie's house. Lacey was with Louis when they arrived. Dexter looked like always, except his coveralls were new. He turned the Belgian loose in the front meadow and joined the other two men on the porch. Lacey followed the men as far as the iron door.

Talon got the key from its hanging nail above the door to the original cabin. He unlocked the iron door and leaned it back against the wall. It was heavy, and creaked as the hinges gave way and let the door lift open. She watched until they descended into the hole and disappeared into the cave.

The memory of the darkness was still fresh in her mind and she had no plans of following any farther. She had a worried look on her face as she turned back to face Aggie and walked outside. The women decided to wait for the explosion in the front meadow. It was closer to the door in case of bad news.

Talon led the way into the shaft and up through the ceiling hole. Dexter was a little uneasy about being in the cave when it blew and began to think of how to deal with it.

Once they got into the long straight lava tube that Jeff had found, Talon led them down the tube about a hundred feet from the hole and stopped. "Not sure where is best," he said. "I just want to close it up tight enough to stop anyone getting through it. Dexter looked around with the light Talon had given him.

The tube was not tall, only about eight feet or so high and maybe twelve feet wide. He could reach the ceiling standing flat footed and checked along it for a way, looking for a place that looked potential. After he walked a few more feet he found what looked like a good spot to him.

The ceiling had a crack about four inches wide and six feet long in it. He shined the light up into the crack and saw that the crack was not straight up. It bent out of sight. It was a crack in lava rock and he hoped it wasn't solid above what he could see.

"How much fuse you got?" Dexter asked Talon.

"I got ten feet. Joseph said it should be enough."

"It's enough," said Dexter. "Where's the caps?"

Talon handed the caps and fuse to Dexter, along with the dynamite. Dexter looked up at the crack again, then he cut two lengths of fuse cord one foot long. He laid the two pieces together to be sure they were the same length, and tied them to the main line and then to the caps. When he was ready, he counted how many feet of fuse he had left. It was foot-a-minute fuse and he cut six feet of it off. He shined his light over at Talon and Louis and checked for matches.

"You two get outa here," he said.

Talon looked over at Louis not sure what to do. He didn't like leaving Dexter alone in the shaft.

"Go on now," said Dexter in a gentle voice. "I don't want anyone in my way getting out of here. Talon could see the reasoning. The thought of being run over by Dexter was all the prompting he needed. Talon and Louis waited with the girls in front of the house. Time ticked by and five or so minutes later Dexter came up.

"That's it?" Louis asked when he saw him.

Dexter smiled and brushed the dust from climbing down through the hole off his clothes. Then he walked over and caught up the lead rope on his horse. He looked down at the pocket watch in his hand and looked up again. In that instant, the ground rumbled and a sound like thunder seemed to start over by the river. It was deep and not easy to hear. Talon was amazed at how deep it sounded. If they had not been listening, they might have missed it altogether.

That evening Talon crept back into the shaft to be sure they had done a good job. The shaft was sealed off tight, with large chunks of riprap piled deep in the shaft. Some of it was of the quartz-looking stuff he had seen in some of the older part of the cave. He realized he had blown out the floor of another shaft but the shaft was not accessible. Whatever else it did, he didn't care. The tube was closed forever. It was a very satisfying feeling.

"Mark that with chalk," Talon said in a low voice. He went back up and sat down to supper.

Chapter 26

A Cat in a Corner

Jeff Baker was panning gold in the little waterfall when the charge blew. The mountain made noises all the time but they were more like groaning or whining noises. Now and then he could hear what sounded like a falling rock, but this was different. It came without a warning. It was also too distant to be heard if it hadn't been so loud. It sounded like somewhere deep in the mountain the ceiling had fallen.

The sound of the little stream almost drowned it out. If he had not been standing at the time he might not have heard it at all. He stood and listened for a little while and decided something must have happened in one of the caves that joined the area he had marked. It was a long walk, but he knew his way and the more he thought about it the more he wanted to know. If it blocked his way to Talon's place it was a game changer and that would not do at all.

He replayed the sound in his head until he went to sleep that night. The more he thought about it the more it bothered him. Saturday morning after he ate he set out up the shaft.

The day before the blast, Jeff had been to town at the courthouse. He had paid for a claim on his little stream, and he had filled out a land sale application he had learned about from researching federal land auction records.

He got the idea from talking to old Jolly. Jolly knew some things about the reservation that had been forgotten. The information he got from him turned out to be correct. Things were starting to lean in his favor. He filled out the application and mailed it off.

It was late Saturday when Jeff got back to town. The hotel was closed but he let himself in through the back door. Lacey was not in the lobby and it was dark. He let the swinging doors close from full open, hoping to get her attention. He assumed she was in her room. Lacey's room was on the second floor just above the porch that overlooked the street.

She heard the doors close and swing back and forth until they stopped moving. She suspected it was Jeff, but wasn't sure. She knew he would be around as soon as he found the cave-in. She hoped he would think it was natural. Caves, she thought, often caved in.

She crept down the single flight of stairs into the cooking area and slipped past the stove without a sound. When she was close enough to see through the counter window she saw that she was right. Jeff was standing by her favorite table facing the kitchen. He caught her movement in the dark. She was wearing a bathrobe with her nightgown under it.

"So!" said Jeff. He was almost yelling. "Your Indian buddy must have quite a curiosity. Must be wandering around in the cave these days."

She knew what he was talking about, but wasn't offering up anything. She walked out of the kitchen door slowly, keeping her eyes on Jeff. She was trying to read his body language. He looked mad enough to be dangerous.

"Spose he does?" She walked over to her table and sat down. Jeff was still standing. He pulled a piece of coarse red paper about the size of half a dollar bill from his pocket and tossed it at her. The paper was heavy and slid across the table to where she sat. She folded her arms and ignored it.

Jeff leaned over the table on both hands to get as close to her face as he could. He smelled of sweat and had mud marks from where it had run down the temples of his face. His face was red. She supposed it was from anger. He looked mad.

"You told him didn't you?" Jeff said

She suspected the paper was what they wrap dynamite in, but even if not it was something like it. At any rate, she knew that he found out the shaft had been blasted shut.

"Talon is my friend, Jeff," she said, "but I wouldn't offer up my whole life for him."

"You're lying!" He said. "He blasted the shaft shut because you told him it was me in his cave."

He stood back up and glared at her. She glared back. She wasn't threatened by Jeff anymore. He was a problem and a big one, but she knew he had not forgotten Louis. After a second, he began to realize she was not afraid. He pulled out the chair opposite her and sat down. He leaned back and tipped his hat up in the front. He was smiling. It was not a happy looking smile.

"Well, fortunately for me," he said, "it don't matter. You see, I've been over to the courthouse and learned a few things about the reservation a lot of people don't know. It turns out that your Indian buddy's house is not his."

Lacey had heard all the stories of the haunted cabin and knew from Aggie how it came to be Talon's. She also knew Talon had some sort of paper from the Nez Perce that made the cabin his, so she wondered what Jeff might be talking about. She said nothing and waited for Jeff to finish.

"Seems that back in ninety-three the reservation was busted up. Land that had Indians on it was kept as reservation. The rest was sold to anyone with a little money. Your buddy's cabin was considered excess land, but it got overlooked because it had a cabin on it. The filing date expired, as you must have guessed, but because it was for sale and not sold I filed to buy it. Chances are very good that the Fed is going to sell it to me."

Lacey didn't know if he was desperate enough to lie or if he really had filed on Talon and Aggie's land. "Talon will file on squatter's rights. You won't stand a chance in court. Anyway, if you do get the go ahead, what makes you think I won't tell the sheriff that you admitted to setting the fire in this hotel? I think you might have killed that insurance man too." Talon had told her of Douglas Brogan. He was having his own suspicions about Jeff and Brogan. She was desperate. She knew she had nothing more than her word to tell the sheriff but she was being backed into a corner.

"I thought of that," said Jeff. "I wondered if you might draw that conclusion, but it's really only your word against mine. And mine is a lot easier to believe." He reached into his coat pocket and pulled out a small box of matches he tossed onto the table. "I think these belong to you," he said.

He didn't have to explain anything. She knew what he was suggesting. She sat and said nothing. She had nothing to say. She knew he could make it look like she was guilty. He might be able to take Talon's cabin as well, but she doubted it. He could raise enough of a stink in town about her and Talon to be a serious threat though.

"That would be kind of a hard sell, don't you think?" she asked.

"Maybe," Jeff said, "or maybe not. But we won't have to find out if you just give me a little slack. You should remember how much of your relationship with this town, and especially the smithy, I can destroy, Lacey. If I can't get that gold any other way, I will burn Talon's pretty little house to the ground."

"I'm not stupid, Jeff," she said. "There's more to this than gold. I see it in your face every time you mention his name. You hate him. You don't even know him, and you hate him."

"I know him, Lacey," said Jeff. "He made a fool out of me, and cost me a fine rifle. That only happens once. I am now prepared to do anything I can think of. He owes me and I'm taking it in gold. All you have to do is tell me. I know you have been talking to his wife and you know more than you are telling me. So this is my last offer.

"I know they go to church on Sunday, every Sunday. That iron door can't be that hard to find. All you need to do is tell me where to go from there. If you lie, I will be back and I will stop at nothing to make you regret it."

Lacey had no doubts about what he was saying. She was desperate now. He would do everything he said. If she sent him out and he lived, he would consider the gold a loss, and his vengeance would be as cruel as being skinned alive. Jeffery Baker was a lot of things, but a fool wasn't one of them, and he wasn't a man afraid to do what he wanted if he wanted.

"I'm going to tell you what I know," said Lacey. "It's all I know. If it's not enough there is nothing more you can learn from me. I'm telling you this on one condition. I don't want any of the gold. I just want you to tell me you will leave me, and my friends, alone forever. I won't tell you one word on any other terms. Her voice was cold and so were her eyes. She hated everything about Jeff. She especially hated being beaten by him.

"Tell me," said Jeff

"Do you agree?" Lacey asked.

"If it's all you have, I agree."

She knew he was lying. If he thought it would

help, he would break a promise as fast as swatting a mosquito, but it was all she could do.

"I don't know if they lock the house door or not," said Lacey, "I do know that the iron door is in the left side of the house. Once you are in you will see an old door on the left. It isn't locked. Inside that door, you will see the iron door in the floor right in front of you. It has a strong lock on it. The key is above the door to the room on your right. I've been in the cave. Talon and Aggie took us down there.

"They showed us how they left the cave under the house. The way they took is to the right from the stream. You climb up onto a little bench and not too far later you will find a sort of trench. It's natural like it was washed out or something. At the end of that little trench is a sharp stone that weighs a couple hundred pounds pointing down from the top of the little shaft.

"You will need a jack to push it out. From there they said you will be in another part of the cave.

Follow it to your right, and stay in that shaft for about three miles. At the other end, they couldn't be sure what it looks like. Just follow their tracks and keep the wind in your face and listen for a lot of water. There is a great river way down in the mountain. The gold is at the great river."

Jeff wrote down everything Lacey told him. It all sounded right. He remembered the little bench but he had not explored it. He looked at Lacey. She looked as calm as a cat. He shook his head a little and smiled.

"You're a good girl," he said, "I don't believe I will ever be back."

Lacey followed Jeff through the swinging doors into the back room. She was thinking of being able to dig the clay out of the latch and was glad she could finally be rid of the problem of Jeff Baker.

CHAPTER 27

PROBLEM SOLVED

Sunday morning came with a clear sky and warm air. Lacey could see the river from the window in her room. She was still tired and felt a little cold. It had been a long night, and she hadn't slept. She sat on her bed Indian-fashion and held a cup of coffee in both hands.

She hated herself for what she had had to do, but it was done and there was no going back, even if she wanted to. She lowered her head and let her long blond hair hide her in that safe little closet she knew so well.

Then she cried again. She knew she needed to get hold of her emotions, but it was nearly impossible. She kept telling herself it was over now. He was gone, and she still had her life to live.

She lifted her head when she heard a wagon on the street. It was Talon and Aggie on their way to church. She was thinking of starting to go to church. Louis might even go with her. It made her feel a little better. Maybe God would forgive her. She couldn't forgive herself, at least not yet. Maybe someday.

The curtain was pulled mostly shut except for a place a few inches wide in the middle and they couldn't see her. Aggie looked over at the hotel but it looked like it always did on Sunday, closed and abandoned.

Church was the highlight of the week for most folks in town, and today they were having a potluck dinner outside after the service. Reed left Shadow tied to one of the wheels on the wagon. He fidgeted and whined at everyone who passed and because he was cute and sociable he got a few pats on the head.

It was mid-afternoon by the time the dinner broke up and Talon loaded the wagon. The ride up the river was quiet and nice. Everything that made the Idaho mountains beautiful was on display and Reed noticed it all, and pointed it out to his parents. He even showed some of it to Shadow, who had no idea what it was about but looked in the direction he was pointing anyway.

The instant they crossed the bridge, Talon stopped the wagon. He studied the house as he pulled the 38 from its holster and checked the load. Everything seemed normal except for one major thing. A strange horse was in the front meadow with his horses. Aggie looked over at Talon. She didn't know who the horse belonged to, but she knew it wasn't one of theirs.

"That's Jeff Baker's horse," said Talon. "Stay here with Reed." He turned the wagon around in the meadow so it was facing out. "Keep watch on the door," he told her. "If I ain't the first man you see coming out, you hightail it for town."

Lacey wished she had the shotgun. They had been caught totally off guard. She grabbed Talon's arm as he started to get off the wagon. His eyes told her it would be okay. She wasn't that convinced.

Talon checked the front door. It was still locked. Then he noticed the window next to the door. It was broke entirely out. Careful attention had been taken to remove all the glass in the edges, no doubt for safe entry. He unlocked the door and slipped in soundlessly. The door to the original cabin was open and he could see the iron door was also open. The lock lay on the floor with the key still in it.

As quietly as he could he picked up one of the flashlights near the door and crept down the stairs. There was no light in the shaft so he turned his on. He stopped to listen. No sound came from the shaft other than the wind. There were tracks in the floor but he couldn't tell whose they were. Domingo and Louis had been in there, and some of them might be his. He couldn't tell much in the loose ground.

He searched the shaft but found nobody. When he was satisfied with the cave he climbed the stairs as silently as a cat. As he passed the front door he opened it and looked out. Aggie was still in the wagon. He motioned to her to stay there.

Step by step he checked every corner of the house. There was no one. Jeff was gone. If he was in the cave the mountain, had him now, Talon reasoned. He put the 38 away and went to get Aggie and Reed from the wagon.

Aggie made him lock the iron door again and this time she kept the key herself, it was the only way she felt safe.

Lacey hurried down the street. It was late in the day and Louis had already been up and around for quite a while. She ran to him when she saw him and threw herself into his arms. He could see she had been crying.

"Lacey?" Louis said.

"It's okay," she said. "Just another visit from Jeff. The last one."

Louis was instantly angry. Jeff had overstepped his bounds the last time and it was time to set things straight. He didn't ask what happened, he could see she was not physically hurt. He could also see she had been crying. It made his blood run cold. He had never thought of killing a man before, but this was Lacey. He knew he could kill for her.

"Where is he?" His voice was as cold as the stone gray of his eyes.

Lacey knew what was on his mind. She needed this moment and didn't care about anything else.

"Gone," she said. She squeezed him tighter.

"I'm going to find him," said Louis.

"He didn't hurt me, just more threats." Then she started crying again.

"I'm done with Jeff, Lacey. No more."

Louis started thinking things out. He needed a way to catch a weasel. He wasn't sure how he would do it, but he would find a way. Jeff had caused all the tears he ever would for Lacey, or Louis couldn't think of himself as a man anymore.

She had stopped crying again and Louis started walking her back to the hotel. They were passing the sheriff's office before Lacey looked up from the ground. She was holding Louis's hand and hadn't noticed Talon and Aggie were there. Talon was just getting down from the wagon. He didn't look very happy. "Hey Louis," he said, "you look like we both had a day of it."

"You got trouble?" Louis asked.

"Someone broke into our house. I think they are in the cave. I think it was Jeff; his horse was left in our yard." Jeff's horse was tied to the back of the wagon. "We brought him in to the sheriff. If he did what I think he did, he won't be back."

Lacey looked bad to Talon. He had never seen her like this before. Her dress was wrinkled and had dust and dirt on it and her hair, though tied up, had begun to come out of the bun. She looked like she had been dragged by a horse.

"Did he hurt you?" Talon asked

"No," she said, "but he was going to. He was going to hurt all of us."

"He went into the mountain," said Talon. "He won't be back and if he does, he'll find himself in a prison cell. The door's locked from the outside.

It was obvious that Lacey had been crying. Talon had never seen her cry before. She always just bulled up and braced for a fight. She looked broken. Her eyes were still red. She clung to Louis's hand with both of hers. He thought she couldn't have looked more beaten had she been raped.

"This is nothing to do with you," Talon told Lacey, "Jeff is a fool, and soon enough he'll be a dead fool. I don't even feel sorry for him."

Lacey looked up at Talon and tried to smile. It looked almost as bad as if she hadn't tried. He was more than just a friend to her. She had no words for what he meant to her, but she was glad things had ended well. Louis was feeling like he needed to be doing something, but he couldn't tell what.

"Sheriff ain't here on Sunday," said Louis. "Probably should just take the horse over to the stable for now. Leave him there. Dennis will find him in the morning."

Talon had forgotten it was Sunday, and realized Louis's idea was a good one.

Aggie got down from the wagon, and went to Lacey. She put her arms around her for a moment. In a little while, she led Lacey back toward the hotel. She looked over at Talon.

"We need coffee," she said.

Coffee, thought Lacey. That was exactly what she needed.

Chapter 28

The Claybank was Packin

Lacey and Louis were married on the rock at Louis's fishing hole three days later. It wasn't a big party, but the people who mattered were there. Aggie's father and mother even came.

Louis had commissioned a photographer in from Bear Valley, and the old preacher from the town church did the service. Lacey ordered her dress the week before. It was white, and had a long train with small lead crystals sewn into the neck and waist seam. In the late summer sun the crystals glittered in the sun, and cast little rainbow colors of light that moved across the air and colored anything they touched.

Louis wore a suit for the first time in his life and new boots. His suit was black with tiny emerald green stripes that ran up and down on it.

They appeared the perfect couple. It was a fairy-tale wedding, and Aggie knew it was one she would always remember. She had become best friends with Lacey, and was proud of her decision to marry Louis.

Summer was fading a little, and some of the leaves were changing color. Aggie stood and watched the trail from the large flat rock. She re-membered every corner in it. It made her feel glad it was her home. She also felt glad for Louis and Lacey. When Lacey threw the bouquet, May fum-bled the catch and almost lost it in the river. It landed in the water just offshore and she waded out and got it.

After the wedding, Talon and Aggie stood with Louis and Lacey for a portrait that hung for the rest of Lacey's life in the lobby of the hotel.

Geese and ducks came by for a look and song-birds sang all the music that they had that day. There was laughter and food, and for a moment the world seemed perfect.

The small party broke up around three in the afternoon, and Talon and Aggie went home by way of the old trail that led past her parents' house. Aggie couldn't resist a home visit, and they stayed until dark.

On Friday an unexpected thing happened that was just what Axle was waiting for. Larry Adams came back to town. He had been in Boise looking for a good business venture but hadn't found anything and decided to try farther north. He stopped by Cougar Rock on his way to Billings. He only meant to stay for a night or two and maybe leave his horses there so he could take the stage. He was not a trail man and was getting tired of the saddle.

The horse that belonged to Jeff Baker was in the corral when Dennis found it and thought Jeff had left it. He only discovered the truth when Seth told him. The horse was in bad need of shoes. Normally it would have been ignored, but Seth had made friends with the horse and liked him. Seth had heard that Jeff had gone into the mountain and figured that if he never came back, he might like to buy the horse from the city. It really wasn't much of a horse, but he had no other, and he thought he liked this one. He paid Louis to do the work. Louis had the horse tied to a hitching post in front of the Anvil.

It was mid-afternoon when Larry Adams rounded the big ponderosa pine and started down Main Street. The street was littered with people and buggies. The feral dogs in town were in the shade of the pine and got up to follow him into town.

He had been fed up with Cougar Rock but now he had a good feeling about being back. It was a familiar feeling, like he belonged there, even if he did go someplace else. He rode into town with the packhorse in tow and a smile on his face. The saloon looked just like it always had. There was even old Jolly leaned back sleeping in a chair up against the wall, under the awning.

Dan Lampwick in a freight wagon caught up and passed Larry on his way back to the sawmill for another load of lumber, and Larry waved when he recognized him. Dan looked a little surprised and waved back. Even the dust seemed a welcome sight.

Doves flew down from the tops of the buildings to look for anything they could find on the ground and flew back up if anyone got too close. It felt good to be back.

The packhorse Larry had was a claybank color and not a bad looking horse. Larry rode past the Anvil on his way to the West Branch where he planned to get a room for his stay in town.

As he passed the Anvil, Jeff's horse suddenly tossed his head in the air and started neighing at Larry. The horse braced himself on his hind legs and pulled back hard on the lead to his halter. The hitching rail pulled loose, and the rope with it. Louis tried to grab the lead rope when he saw what was happening, but was too late. Jeff's horse made a straight run at Larry. The claybank also started a homecoming song when it saw Jeff's horse.

Larry spurred his saddle horse to make him move a little faster, but Jeff's horse had already caught up. He was nudging the claybank and keeping step with him. It was the strangest thing either man had ever seen. Somehow Jeff's horse knew the claybank and knew him well.

Larry, not knowing what else to do, turned around in the street and rode back to the Anvil. He wasn't sure what was going on at first, but when he took a closer look he remembered where he had seen Jeff's horse before.

Louis was not happy. He had the hitching rail in his hand and was wondering how he could fix it.

"We maybe should just build another one," said Dexter. "We could make it out of iron this time. Can't pull that apart."

The idea was a good one for two reasons. First, he could get Dexter to do it and second Dexter was right. *In fact,* thought Louis, *we could cement it in. It will be here when the Lord returns.* The idea made him feel a little better. "That's a right good idea," Louis said, "get right on it."

Dexter smiled. He had come to like working with iron, and it was a simple project.

Larry had stopped in the street waiting for someone to notice he had Jeff's horse and take it back from him. Louis turned to address that very thing. "I have no idea what Seth wants with that horse," he said. "If it were up to me, I'd shoot him dead here in the street."

To make matters worse, Jeff's horse seemed to have a sort of smile on its face. Louis wished he could slap it off of him.

"Get the nuisance back over to the stable if you can, and I can put him in a corral." He looked up, and for the first time realized who he was talking to.

"Well," he said, "if it ain't Larry Adams. I thought

you flew the coop for good. Hope you ain't come to buy the hotel back again, cause I can tell ya it ain't for sale."

"Nope," said Larry, "just passing through, if I can get shed of that fella's horse, that is."

"You know that horse do ya?" Louis asked.

"Well if I ain't mistaken," said Larry, "that's the horse the fella rode who sold me this here pack-horse. Good thing that horse has a memory, cause he sure ain't got nothin else to brag about. That fella still around, is he?"

"Not sure, if that makes any sense," said Louis. "Could be he ain't comin back for this horse anyway. Folks think he got himself lost inside the mountain."

"Well that's too bad," said Larry, "seemed like a nice sorta guy when he sold me this horse."

Louis was looking at the claybank. He looked familiar. It was an odd color horse and not often seen. He caught up to Jeff's horse and walked him across the street to the stable where he tied him to the hitching rail on that side.

Dennis saw him and assumed he had finished the foot work Seth had asked for. He came out to put the horse away. Dennis wasn't a big man, but he was a bit of a fat one. He was a little under six feet, and weighed around three hundred pounds. He was wearing blue denim jeans and a funny looking little brown hat that Louis thought made him look Irish. His shirt was made of blue cotton. He had a full beard and kept it groomed. He even sported a handlebar mustache that made his already round face look even more round.

Larry waited for Louis to come back. He was interested in what happened to Jeff. Dennis caught up with Louis before he got the horse tied.

"All done?" Dennis asked.

"Not yet," said Louis, "pulled free." Louis wasn't looking at Dennis he was looking at the claybank. "You ever seen that horse before?" Louis asked.

Dennis noticed the other horse for the first time. He looked a little interested like he was trying to place where he had seen him. "Ya, maybe I have," he said. He walked across the street to the claybank. Larry watched with curiosity as Dennis approached. The horse had kept Dennis preoccupied and he had not noticed Larry. He looked up and saw him as he approached.

"Well, looky here," said Dennis. "It's our ol buddy Larry Adams, come home to Cougar Rock. Ain't you a travelin man. Good to see ya."

Larry liked being recognized as part of the town. He wasn't planning to stay, but he was glad he dropped by.

"Hey Dennis," said Larry. "You like that claybank? You might be keepin him for me a while."

"Ya, I kinda do like him," said Dennis. "I think I know him too. Don't he have a heart-shaped saddle-sore scar on his left shoulder."

Larry's pack had the spot covered. "Well in fact he does," Larry said. "Not big, but a perfect heart shape. Kinda odd."

"Yep, I know him," said Dennis. "Belonged to that insurance man who sold me my insurance.

Spose that was wasted money. That fella's dead; how is it you got his horse?"

Larry didn't like the way they were so interested in the horse. He reminded himself that he was back in Cougar Rock. Trouble seemed to always find him in Cougar Rock. He didn't know what the big deal was yet, but he didn't trust how he had suddenly become the center of attention.

"Bought him off a tall blond miner the day I left," said Larry. You sure it's the same horse?"

"Same horse," said Dennis, "kept him here for a month or more. That's him alright."

Once Dennis pegged the horse, Louis remembered him as well. He had seen him in the stable corral every time he looked over across the street for anything. The horse stood out. He remembered him well. He hadn't known who he belonged to, but it made sense it was Brogan's horse.

"You got a little time?" Louis asked Larry. "Sheriff needs to see this horse."

"Well I spose I have to," Said Larry, "but I ain't

gonna like it if my trip gets delayed."

He was back home alright. Back to the same old small town stuff he thought he had left behind. He stepped down from his horse and ground-tied him. Louis looked over at Dexter and motioned him over.

"If you wouldn't mind," he asked Dexter, "could you run up the street and bring Domingo Wells down here?"

"Well sure I can," said Dexter, "but why don't he just ride up there?"

"Well he could," said Louis, "if we was to shoot that knot-head that already tore half the city down trying to follow him the first time."

Dexter wanted to ask why they didn't just pen Jeff's horse, but could see that an argument was developing. The sheriff's office was little less than a block away and it seemed faster to just go get him. He had just gotten started on the iron hitching post, and hated being interrupted, but figured maybe a walk would do him good. He hoped the Sheriff was in his office.

Domingo and Axle were both there and walked back down with Dexter. They looked over the two horses and talked to Larry about staying around until things could be settled.

"Told ya he would let us know when it was time to hang him," said Axle. "Now, if we can find him."

The sheriff and Axle started back for the office and Larry set out for the hotel. He wondered what else Cougar Rock would throw at him there. He and that hotel had never been the best of friends.

"When was the last time you saw Baker?" Domingo asked Axle.

"Well," said Axle, "not since before we got his horse. Could be, he really 'is' in the mountain. Word has it Lacey Clanton was the last one to see Baker."

"Guess we should see Lacey in that case," said Domingo, "and find out what she knows. Might be interesting to see how far she thinks he went, and if he's coming back."

When the two men arrived at the hotel, they were only a few minutes behind Larry. Lacey was standing in the lobby with her arms folded across her chest, staring at Larry. She looked a little less than entertained. Larry was standing in front of her. He looked as upset as he ever had and was trying to defend his position.

"I never even thought about that investigation thing," said Larry, "I just wanted out. Can't you just give me a room and let me rest a little? I'm sorry you think I was trying to pull somethin, but it don't matter now anyway, does it? You made a modern-day moneymaker out of this place."

He could see steam rising off the water. Seth was washing dishes a few yards away in the kitchen. "Look at that," he said, "you even found a way to get hot water in here. I don't see what you got to worry about."

Domingo was mildly interested in the conversation, but not enough to hear the last of it. He stepped closer to Larry and interrupted them. "Lacey," he said, "I need a word with you."

Lacey looked a little worried. She had never

been the interest of a sheriff before. She wondered if Jeff had told Domingo something she would not be able to refute. She walked over to the key board and pulled down one of the room keys. She handed it to Larry, who without another word took the key and headed for the stairs. Seth took a moment and retrieved Larry's bags from the boardwalk and took them to his room.

"You like coffee?" Lacey asked Domingo.

"Turns out I would," said Domingo.

Lacey left and in a minute returned with cups and coffee.

"We're looking for Jeff Baker," said Domingo.

"Checked the outhouse?" asked Lacey. "It's getting cold out; he might of decided he needed a room."

Domingo smiled, he would have laughed but he was trying to stay on track. "Not yet," he said, "we heard you might know more than we do bout that."

"Well I don't," said Lacey, "I try to avoid sick people."

Domingo caught the pun. She wasn't saying Jeff was ill.

"Well," said Domingo, "rumor has it you had something of a connection to him. Nobody seems to know what, but what we do know is that he visited here a few times late, and now he's gone. His horse showed up at the Windcatcher's place and they brought him in."

Lacey began to get curious. She knew the sheriff had Jeff's horse and that he had been told how Jeff got into the mountain by Talon. It made her wonder why he was sounding like she would know if he had actually gone or not. She hoped he wasn't thinking she had hid him or something. "Can I ask why you want him?" she said, "Not like I care, but it might be interesting."

"Well right now," said Domingo, "we want to question him for murder and arson. We think he's the one who set your hotel on fire."

Lacey could have told him a little about the fire, but the murder was more or less new to her. She suspected it, but had no real reason to actually place blame. Things Jeff had said made her wonder, but she really didn't care.

"Well, he did come by a couple times," said Lacey. "He used to know my mother long ago. I guess he thought I might be like her. I'm not. He told me he knew how to get into Talon's cave and he was going into the mountain to get the gold Talon found there.

"That was a week or so ago. Haven't seen him since, don't want to. However, if he don't ever come back and you are still wanting to hang someone, hang his horse. It would be a mercy."

"Hey!" yelled Seth from the kitchen.

"Hey yourself," Lacey yelled back. "This was supposed to be a private conversation."

Seth realized what he had done, and if he could have turned red he would have. "Sorry," he said. He went back to his dishes.

"Well," said Domingo, "we would sure like to talk to him, so if he does come back we would like to know, day or night."

"I promise," said Lacey, "you'll hear me scream-ing down the boardwalk all the way to your office."

Domingo smiled again. "I'll be listening," he said.

CHAPTER 29

OR IS HE…?

Domingo and Axle walked back to the office in silence. Once there, Domingo pulled his chair over near the wall and sat down. He leaned back against the wall and propped his feet up on the desk.

Axle picked up a newspaper he had sent in from the valley. He sat in his favorite chair in front of the cell. The sun came in through the cell window and made reading easy.

Domingo had his hat pulled down. He was sorting things out. The only sound in the room was a blowfly that maintained an orbit around the ceiling light as if it was on. Domingo's voice broke the otherwise silence. Without opening his eyes he said, "So Axle, what's your take on where Baker is?"

"Well," said Axle, without lowering his paper, "way I see it, he's either in that mountain and won't likely ever not be, or... he's wherever Lacey Clanton found to hide his body."

"Hide his body? You think Lacey might have actually killed him?" Domingo asked. "Even if she could, why would she?"

"I've known Lacey most of her adult life," Axle said. "She's not rebellious but she is determined, and she's not used to being cornered.

"I talked to Jolly over at the saloon. He tells me that Jeff liked to talk when he was drunk. Jeff told Jolly that he had the power to turn this whole town upside down. He didn't say how. Said he had things leaning his way, and it was only a matter of time before he was a rich man.

"From the conversation, it seemed to Jolly that it all had something to do with Lacey Clanton but he couldn't find out what. I also talked to Seth. Seth tells me that Lacey had been in a couple arguments with Jeff after closing hours. He couldn't tell what it was about, but he could hear that it was not friendly. Evidently Seth's room is upstairs in the front. He said as long as they were talking in the lobby he could hear some, but not all.

"He said Lacey hated Jeff from the start. Seth also said that Jeff had the cave marked with chalk way back. He thinks it leads to Talon and Aggie's place. He had more to tell but not to me. Not to anyone as far as I could tell. Way I figure it, Jeff wanted something from Lacey that involved Talon and Aggie. If he was to tell her that she would be implicated in his game if she didn't cooperate, she might become desperate enough to kill him. He had a good line with her happening to land here when she did. He could have used that."

"Well," said Domingo, "I guess it don't matter to me either way. Still, it is interesting. If Jeff figured he was coming back, how I wonder was he planning on getting back through that iron door at Talon's?"

"I don't think he was planning that far ahead," said Axle. "He probably figured he would find a way out later. One mountain at a time. If you want, I can do a little more digging, but you might learn more than you want to know."

"No," said Domingo, "leave it alone. Far as we know he really is in the mountain."

"Well in that case," said Axle, "allow me to quote the famous Seth Jackson just one more time: 'I'm hungry.' See you up at the West Branch."

Did you enjoy this book?

We need your help! Your honest opinion is the most effective tool we have to get the word out about Don's books. Reviews are the number one thing readers rely on when looking at a book by an author they have not read before. If you will take just a few minutes and give your honest opinion of this book on Amazon, Goodreads, or your favorite book site, it will make a huge difference. Thank you.

Inheriting the Missing

Under the Flowers is Book 3 in the Windcatcher series. Book 1, *Inheriting the Missing*, is the story of Talon's journey to Cougar Rock.

They thought he was a runaway Indian or a criminal, but it was the only chance he had. If he succeeded, the world was his; if not, no one would ever look for his body.

Talon had one round of ammunition, two good horses, and little else. He was nineteen years old and life as he knew it had come to a close. A thousand miles away lay the only thing that looked like a future to him.

If he survived the trip, the land and cabin he had inherited were famous among the nations for being a place of the dead — where people went in, but they never came out. It was all he had. It was enough to drive him to challenge one thousand miles of trail he had never seen, through a world he had only heard stories of. His only plan was to make a plan as he went.

The first one to take up his trail he wasn't too worried about — her he could handle. The posse was not as easy to ignore. If you can't outrun your enemy, then you'd better be able to out-think them.

THE WINDCATCHER'S CAVE

In *The Windcatcher's Cave*, book 2 in the Windcatcher series, Talon and his neighbor Aggie are trapped when she is chased into the cave by a bear with no intention of letting them go.

The long shadow that filled the doorway was all she needed to know that the bear was still behind her. Bruised and dazed she ran for her life into the total darkness of the cave. The dull thud of the bear hitting the ground in the entry let her know he was not giving up.

Aggie Stonewell was not supposed to be there. She was a good girl from a good family, and it was such a harmless little lie. Where it took her was beyond belief. Into miles of interlocking caves, with a man she had only seen from a distance. Feeling their way in the total absence of light, through stone structures and sulfur springs in the deep, dark, dampness of a massive cave whose only sound was the constant wind and the occasional moan of the bear that had nowhere else to be.

In the outside world, the ground echoed with the sound of horses' hooves, scouring every inch of forest for miles, desperate to find a young woman lost someplace in the Sawtooth, a land that rarely gives up it's dead.

All three books in the Windcatcher series are available in paperback, eBook, and large-print versions. Buy Now to start reading. You can visit our website at tazlinaglacier.com for information on purchasing them in person or online.

Staying in Touch

To receive notice of news or special offers related to Don's books, join our email list at

https://tazlinaglacier.com/email/

Our publishing company website:

https://tazlinaglacier.com

Donald Hofstetter, Author Facebook page:

https://www.facebook.com/donaldhofstetter/

Don's Instragram page with pictures of Alaska, Idaho, and the things he most enjoyed:

https://www.instagram.com/
donaldhofstetter_alaska_idaho/

Email to: thofstetter@tazlinaglacier.com